Pinky Swears

By Shea Warner

Copyright © 2020 Shea Warner All rights reserved

The characters and events portrayed in this book are fictitious. Any similarity to real persons, living or dead, is coincidental and not intended by the author.

No part of this book may be reproduced, or stored in a retrieval system, or transmitted in any form or by any means, electronic, mechanical, photocopying, recording, or otherwise, without express written permission of the publisher.

ISBN-13: 9798690571245

Cover design by: Shea Warner
Library of Congress Control Number: 2018675309
Printed in the United States of America

What did my fingers do before they held him?

    -Sylvia Plath

Pinky Swears

By Shea Warner

1. february 29th.

i never really liked this movie. i don't know why i lied to you. los angeles still isn't as kind as i thought it'd be. it's disconcerting, seeing you in a summer dress when it's snowing back home.

(no matter how many rent payments we've made, this isn't home.)

i dream of going back, but i'll need at least six more songs before i can even think about a plane ticket. tonight we'll fall asleep to the santa ana winds whispering in our ears and the neighbor's dog whining for no apparent reason. and above all, we'll try not to think about the widening gap between us. there's something so dishonest about this city,

but somehow the day that only comes every four years contains more truths than any other.

2. those types of people.

i suppose you didn't give much thought to your name until me. i'm sure you told your sister all about this strange specimen you came across two blocks from wrigley, this *girl* named evan.

you sat in the restaurant from opening to closing, tapping your fingers along to the kanun music. you rarely ordered anything (still deciding, of course) and my boss kept telling me to ask you to leave.

i never did. i could always tell that place inspired you, the batik drapes and the frankincense. you were always hard at work on something, scribbling in a notebook.

on the tenth day, you finally ordered mint tea and a hummus platter.

hey, you said, motioning to my nametag. *my name is evan too.* i laughed nervously.

oh, sorry, you continued. *i guess this just got awkward.*

well, actually, my entire life was awkward, because i was the lone white employee at a shawarma restaurant and possibly the only person from my graduating class who had yet to get a real job, even a sellout-y corporate one.

i just laughed again (i've never been all that articulate, as you know) and said, *well, it's more awkward that my parents gave me a boy name.*

before i left your table, you asked me if that was my natural hair color. i said yes. you smiled, pushed your glasses further up the bridge of your nose, and said *til we meet again, evan.*

that night, for the first time in my life, i actually fell asleep looking forward to tomorrow.

3. crimson glow.

your hair isn't as red as it used to be. i guess i always suspected you were lying. i found a box under the sink, and i got a little more mad than i should've.

it's for grays, you insisted.

bullshit, you're thirty, i replied.

but i guess we all try to see how long we can keep something a secret, whether it's the fact i had to repeat fifth grade (*it's hard for everyone*, they assured me, trying to make me hate everything a little less) or the fact you lied a bit about your hair color.

but hey, when you're thirty and still wearing a nametag to work, i can see why you'd want to protect yourself. lies are like warm blankets in the bitterest of winters.

4. childhood fantasies.

i saw you the next day, and the next, and the next. evan. *boy evan.* slumped over a marble composition book, chewing your pencil and squinting at the page. i guess you needed stronger glasses. i was under stern orders to kick you out. biting my lip, i walked towards your table.

my boss says you have to order something or leave, i said softly. you looked up.

i'll take a turkey shawarma sandwich, you said. *and your number.*

i floated for the rest of the day. my roommate told me i was getting ahead of myself.

he's probably a creep, she said, picking at the green polish on her toenails. i just giggled, thinking of the guitar case that had been resting at your feet.

ever since i was little, i had wanted to marry a musician.

5. microwaving my sister's malibu barbies.

you've adapted quite well to california. better than i have, and *i* was the reason we had to move here in the first place. but i miss chicago. i miss the breezes off lake michigan and walking through oak park and watching cubs games. i miss the shawarma restaurant, because it was easier there.

i'd say i miss new jersey, that i miss my aunt and uncle, that i miss my sister, but i don't even know if i'd be lying.

a record deal only stressed me out, but it made you tanner. back in illinois, you were the alabaster irish-jewish girl i fell in love with. now you're lightly toasted and i really don't like the way those jackie o sunglasses look on you but i guess i'll just have to put it in a song like i do with every emotion i have nowadays.

6. secure materials.

we just *talked*, honestly. you didn't ask me out, and i was growing goddamned sick of just being the girl friend instead of *the girlfriend*. but still we talked, picking up where we left off.

you told me about all the songs you were writing, the demo tapes you were sending. you told me about growing up in new jersey, houses down the shore and italian hot dogs. still i didn't know how you wound up in chicago. i guess, for you, new york didn't have the same shine as it did for the rest of us.

you came to the restaurant every day, staying until we locked up. you always wore the same sweater, and it was starting to look dirty. you hadn't shaved in a while. but it wasn't my place, my mother would warn.

one day you were fifty cents short for your tea.

don't worry about it, i whispered. you looked up.

really?

i nodded.

really.

a smile. it was like a crocus blooming through the snow, unexpected and beautiful and hopeful. but it was also delicate, also damaged. still, years later, i'm unsure of how that could be, even though i've already flipped to the back and read the last chapter.

7. toothpaste and orange juice.

another long day at the studio. still not really sure if it was rewarding or not. i came home on the bus (i should really get around to learning how to drive) and nearly sleepwalked through the front door.

you were in the back room, messing around with that perennially-unfinished painting, your hair tied up with a kerchief like a girl in a war-effort poster. i leaned against the threshold, cleared my throat. you looked at me, smiled as though you hadn't seen me in years. i hugged you tight, taking fistfuls of your paint-stained shirt, finding a hint of twenty-five.

you then threw up all over my vans. i'm just pretending i'm not mad.

now i'm downstairs, listening to you moan yourself to sleep, listening to my shoes rumble in the washing machine. i googled it.

i like coming home and then i don't, and i really hope i'm not a bad boyfriend, because i left a glass of water on your nightstand and you haven't taken a sip.

8. never take your own advice.

fatima was starting to notice how often i talked to you at the restaurant. i actually got mad when my boss switched her section and mine. still, you only ordered tea. i watched from the kitchen threshold, crossing my arms, while sharif told me to get a grip.

he's just a boy, he said.

he's my friend, i insisted.

how long ago did you exchange numbers?

two weeks ago.

and he hasn't asked you out?

no.

then a friend is all he's gonna be. now go give table seventeen their tahini.

that night, i got drunk and watched cartoons while my roommate was out on a date. and it wasn't until the morning that i saw your text that said *you looked really nice today.*

9. workaholics.

the next morning, i asked you if you felt better. you just shrugged.

my stomach still hurts.

take the day off, i whispered. *i'm not recording today. we can go to disneyland.*

you sighed.

jesus christ, evan. someone here has to fucking work.

i tried not to take it personally.

we ate cereal in total silence, watching the morning news, while fionna alternated between sitting in your lap and kneading my thigh.

i have to go to the drugstore, you said before leaving, fiddling with your earrings.

what do you need? i asked. *i can pick it up for you.*

no, i'll get it myself, you replied, kissing the back of my head. *have a nice day.*

my sister says i shouldn't be worried. *she probably just ran out of tampons,* she wrote back in an email. *relax.*

is it bad that i'm taking advice from a girl who can't tie her own shoes?

10. spun glass.

my hands wouldn't stop shaking, and i didn't know why. my shift was almost over — different people come in to serve the midnight-snackers — and you were still there, sipping your mint tea, flipping through your notebook.

i bid goodbye to sharif, put on my coat and scarf. as i was walking out, you called out to me.

yes? i asked.

we didn't get to talk tonight, you said.

well, they kept me busy. i have to get home.

sit with me, you offered.

hmm?

sit with me, evan.

i loved the way it rolled off your tongue. when i was young, i hated it. maybe i still hate it. but when you said my name, i just sort of lit up inside and felt like cartwheeling, even though i didn't know how.

so i sat down.

how are you? you asked. i could see myself reflected in your glasses. there were bags under my eyes and my hair was limp.

i shrugged.

okay, i guess. tired, i replied.

at eight-thirty? hoo boy.

i laughed.

well, i've been working all day.

you have a really nice smile, you said.

i pressed my lips together, hiding my teeth.

i don't really think so, i mumbled. you chuckled, looked up at the ceiling.

why are you laughing? i asked, somewhat accusatory, but i was really just sad.

because i'll never get it, you said. *at some point, are girls all told they should never accept compliments?*

i shook my head.

no. i just… i mean, i had braces. and i had my teeth bleached. so it's not like they came like this, honestly.

you nodded.

i get it. i lost thirty pounds last summer.

congratulations. i meant it.

thanks, you said, pulling on the cuff of your sweater. *but, i mean, there's always that fat person like inside you, you know?*

i understand, i said.

you sighed, ran your fingers back through your hair.

would you like to come watch my band perform? we're horrible. please say yes.

i laughed.

i'd love to.

walking out of the restaurant, i felt like cinderella at the ball. mostly because i kept glancing towards my watch and dreading midnight.

11. why i'm getting nothing done.

you threw up again this morning. when i came with a glass of water, you were flipping through your little calendar, the one you kept in the medicine cabinet along with a red magic marker. i knew what it was for. still, approaching thirty, it grosses me out a little.

babe? i asked.

you looked up.

yeah?

i got you water.

you stood up, bracing yourself against the sink. long, silent sips.

you going to work today? i asked.

i have to, you said with a nod.

you're sick, you shouldn't.

i have to work. we can't live off your record advance much longer, you snapped.

i knew it wasn't supposed to be an insult. i knew you were just cranky because it was early and your stomach wasn't behaving. but that doesn't mean i'm not sitting on this city bus, biting my lip and inhaling sharply, because sixteen years ago i was told to never let them see you cry.

before i left, i leaned in to kiss you goodbye, but you put a hand on my chest to stop me.

honey, i did just throw up.

i kissed your forehead. you just stared at the floor.

the palm trees are swaying, people are in flip-flops, and i don't even know what i want right now.

12. the mistake, part one.

we swayed with the el train, colliding into each other with every stop. we laughed, and the other riders looked at us with warm smiles. i suppose we looked like a couple.

how long have you been at the restaurant?

since graduating. clearly art school set me up for a fruitful career.

i'm sure your work is beautiful. there was a strange tightening in my ribcage, and at that point, i didn't know what it was called.

i haven't gotten much time to work lately. i'm always at that damn restaurant. i'm trying to get enough money for my own place.

you live with someone? you suddenly looked apprehensive, as though you feared everything had been in vain.

my friend from college. but she might be moving out soon, she's been going kinda steady with this guy.

you were silent the rest of the ride, adjusting your beanie and staring up at the budweiser ad across the top of the train car.

at the coffeeshop, you introduced me to your bandmates, scott and ivy. she was pretty and i found myself getting jealous for no reason. you introduced me as *my friend evan,* and my heart sunk a little bit. *you're setting yourself up for disappointment,* my roommate kept warning.

the others chuckled, remarking they never thought they'd meet another one, much less a girl one.

evan and evan, they said with smiles, and we laughed with them, trying not to think about how nice a ring it had.

various other acts were getting warmed up. i ordered a latte and sat by the window, staring at gray, gray michigan avenue. snow was falling, the flakes catching the light from skyscrapers. it truly is a beautiful city, forgotten in the shadows of new york and los angeles. we're a city formed on gangsters and ballot stuffing and gritting our teeth and coming out swinging.

the lights went down and the show began. your band was called *between names.* months later i asked if that was a *my so-called life* reference and you just looked at me funny and my heart broke a little. maybe a lot.

you played guitar and sang. i became fascinated with your fingertips against the frets, your clear and honest voice. you were so focused, so absorbed in the words you poured over.

afterwards, while ivy was canoodling with her girlfriend (i had nothing to worry about after all, it seemed), you came up to me, carrying your guitar.

well? you asked, biting your lip.

you were great, i said. *really great.*

honest?

of course. you don't lie to me, so i don't lie to you.

you smiled, raking your fingers back through your hair.

i'm glad you liked it.

did you write those songs in the restaurant?

you nodded.

most of them. the lyrics, at least.

well, when your first album goes platinum, they'll put up a plaque, i'm sure, i said, trying to match your smile.

don't tease me like that, you said. *no one goes platinum anymore anyway.*

i'm not teasing, i insisted. *you want coffee?*

nah, i should… be getting home.

can i walk you there? i offered, standing up and buttoning my coat.

well, uh, we'll have to get back on the el, actually, you admitted, as though you were ashamed. the night was too young to marry, but young nonetheless.

that's okay, i replied. *i have to take it to get back to my place anyway.*

we walked out. i stared up at the sky, humming the songs you had just played, not realizing you were looking at me. i was never good at noticing.

once again, we collided on the train, laughing as it shook on the track, the rhythm all chicagoans quickly pick up on.

we walked down your street in silence, the snow falling heavier. suddenly, you stopped short in front of a doorway, as if you had forgotten where you lived. you looked to me, smiling, clouds of breath fogging your glasses.

well, evan, (a pause to chuckle), *i'm glad you came to see us.*

my pleasure, i answered. *don't forget this place when you get famous.*

you looked around, hands in your pockets.

i don't think i'll have the opportunity, you said, rocking on your heels. you gently reached out to touch my hair. as you took your fingers away, you said, *there was snow in your hair. sorry.*

not a problem, i replied, my boots starting to pivot on the sidewalk, getting ready to leave. *will you be at the restaurant tomorrow?*

you nodded.

where else would i be?

your job? still hadn't asked about that, mostly because i was afraid i already knew the answer.

i walked down the sidewalk, but i didn't hear you opening a door. at the end of the block, i turned around, and saw you walking the opposite way, wrapping your coat tighter around yourself.

evan? i called, jogging down the street, trying to avoid the icy patches. *evan!*

you turned around when i was closer to you, ghost-pale.

evan, i said, breathless. *don't fuck with me, okay? do you not have a place to stay?*

silence. with a sigh, i held out my hand.

come on, i said, beckoning. *you can stay with me.*

you took my hand without a word, just a smile.

13. the bane of our existence.

you came home later than usual, a cvs bag in the crook of your elbow, red-faced, eyes on your shoes. i kissed you hello, all ready to play you the song we had finally finished, but you just went upstairs.

i heard the bathroom door slam shut, and i put my guitar down. still the same one i was playing when you first saw me perform in that chicago hole-in-the-wall, if you remember. of course you do.

just ran out of tampons, i kept chanting in my head, because it was all i could handle.

i started making your favorite meal, grilled cheese and tomato soup. hot food has no place here, but it reminds us of our early days in the city they deemed windy (not that they were wrong, it was just unexpected at first), watching an ice storm while huddled in front of the radiator.

evan? i called up the stairs. *i made dinner. you hungry?*

maybe later, you replied. your voice sounded wobbly, warped. as though you were about to cry. i turned off the stove, climbed up the stairs. knocked on the bathroom door, even as my heart pounded louder.

hon, you okay? i asked.

no, you nearly wailed.

what's wrong? can i come in?

you opened the door with force rivaling the old testament, tracks of mascara striping your cheeks. hyperventilating, you showed me the slim white piece of plastic in your hand, and, in the center, nothing but the word *yes*.

my hands shook as i took it from you, as though it would say anything different if someone else touched it.

shit, i finally forced out.

yeah, you spat, crossing your arms. *shit.*

14. the abstractors.

where's your roommate? you asked as i opened the door.

in colorado, with her parents, i told you. *she likes to ski. i guess you can take her bed, she won't mind.*

you seemed uncomfortable. i felt stupid, mostly.

i opened the fridge.

you want anything to eat? i asked.

you shrugged.

i mean, if you have something.

grilled cheese?

sure.

i made two, one for you and one for me, turned on the television. it was the olympics. snowboarding. you didn't protest. i offered you a beer, but you refused.

fuck, this is a great sandwich, you said, trying to lick the crumbs off your fingers without looking like you were licking the crumbs off your fingers.

why, thank you, i said, feigning flattery. it was just a grilled cheese.

my sister's allergic to, like, everything. i'd like barter at school to get goldfish crackers. my aunt would buy that plasticky kosher cheese but it wasn't the same.

i pushed my hair out of my eyes, tried to watch the tv and look at you at the same time.

you lived with your aunt?

and uncle. my parents died in a car crash when i was eleven.

jesus christ, i'm so sorry, i said, clapping a hand to my chest.

it's not like it's your fault. and my aunt and uncle weren't like evil stepparents or whatever.

you glanced around the living room, focusing on the wall above the tv.

did you paint that? you asked.

i nodded. you were pointing at one of my old paintings my roommate had insisted on hanging up. it was old, from my early days of college, when i was still constantly painting wisconsin landscapes, mostly because i was scared of painting anything else. i had since moved on to rothko-esque smudgy squares.

yeah, i admitted, a little embarrassed.

holy crap. is that of a real place, or —

my family has a cabin in the north woods. wisconsin. that was a the view out the window. in the summer, at least.

it looks like it belongs in a museum.

i blushed.

well, i don't think —

no. accept the compliment, you jokingly scolded, pointing at me. i laughed, pulling my knees to my chest, giving myself a hug.

thank you, i replied, and i meant it.

do you only paint? or, like, do you draw or stuff?

some drawing. illustration and cartoons and stuff. i mean, originally i wanted to get into animation, but it didn't really pan out.

you should totally make album covers and promo posters and stuff. i know a shitload of bands desperate for good logos.

i sighed, arched my back, scratching my neck.

i'm not sure if my work's really ready to be put out there like that.

so you're just gonna spend your life painting stuff to hang above your tv?

i looked to you, pursing my lips, trying to hide a giggle.

well, when you say it like that, i retorted. i couldn't stop smiling and you couldn't either and it was like a drug and i didn't care that some american snowboarder just won a gold medal.

you inched closer to me, until our shoulders were almost touching, and you put your empty plate on the coffee table.

you know the second song i sang?

mhmm. the one that ended something like —

'pinky-swear, fuck 'em all, we'll be happy somewhere else,' you recited.

yeah. what you said, i replied. another dumb giggle. i was suddenly back in high school and i wasn't sure how to feel.

i wrote that hoping you'd hear it someday, you said.

my stomach dropped and my heart started thumping and i felt like something was about to go horribly wrong and right at the same time.

you… did? i stammered.

of course. you're beautiful, evan. you're beautiful and you're talented and you're kind. i mean, no one else in this city would let me stay with them tonight, i'm certain.

i bit my lip, realized how close our hands were to touching.

i put my empty plate on the coffee table, and turned off the tv. gently, without a word, i put a hand on either side of your face, took off your glasses, and kissed you. you kissed back, reaching towards the top button of my blouse.

a mistake rarely shows itself until much later.

15. it has fingernails.

you curled yourself into a little ball on the bed, wearing the afghan my aunt had made us like a cloak, sobbing into the pillow. i laid down next to you, curving my body to fit with yours, hugging you tight as you shook uncontrollably.

evan, it's gonna be all right. you know it is.

it can't be true, you blubbered through your tears. *it has to be a false positive.*

babe, what else could you have missed your period for? i asked quietly.

stop! you wailed. *just stop!*

i bit my tongue. still, i can't edit myself.

we'll go to a doctor. find out for sure.

how did this even happen? you wondered aloud, twisting your class ring, a nervous habit.

i don't know.

i did know. new year's eve. we went to a party and tom had this illegal 140-proof rum from jamaica (the things you get your hands on when your uncle works for the tsa) and it messed us up *really* bad and we definitely had sex in michela's bathtub while we were approximately four miles away from our condoms, because the pill made you weepy and you had a traumatic iud experience in college. i'm not sure who we can really blame.

you bit your lip, looked over your shoulder at me.

evan?

yeah?

will you be mad at me if i keep it? i mean, i'm like pro-choice and shit but i just... i can't will myself to do something like that and —

i won't be mad.

another pause, fingering the delicate stiches along the hem of your t-shirt.

will you stay with me?

of course i will, i whispered, kissing the tip of your ear. your celtic knot earrings were upside-down.

you turned over, looked me straight in the eyes.

swear?

not breaking your gaze, i linked my right pinky with your left. you smiled, ever-so-slightly, through the fear.

16. addictions.

i pulled away, but only by inches, smiling and laughing under my breath.

what is it? you seemed concerned, as though i was laughing at you.

nothing, i replied. *it's just, i've never kissed a guy with a beard before. it's nice.*

you bit your lip.

oh.

i leaned back in, starting to close my eyes.

where were we? i asked in a whisper. you put a hand on my knee, forcing me to pause.

evan, i — are you sure?

why wouldn't i be? i gently touched the side of your face, tilted my head a few degrees.

i haven't been with a lot of women. please don't —

i don't care. it's not about the past. it's just about… tonight. kiss me.

 i knew i was making no sense. i loved how you didn't care.

you did as you were told, kissing me long and hard, letting me bite your bottom lip as you came up for air. you started to unbutton my blouse. before you, i had actually been considering reduction surgery, to rid myself of the backaches and the agony of having to buy bras in plus-size stores. but when i saw the look on your face as i opened my shirt, i guess i, vainly, never thought of wanting to rid myself of double-ds again.

i pulled you to my bedroom, smiling, trying not to be afraid. still there was something scary about someone new, no matter how much experience you had. on the bed, you touched me gently. gentler than any boy at college had treated me. you ran a cold fingertip down my bare stomach and i shivered with a strange ecstasy.

do you have something? i asked, breathless.

hmm?

you know… something.

twenty-five, still speaking in euphemisms.

yeah… just hold on.

you got out of bed, jeans partially off, hair mussed. my heart thumped as i watched you through the open door, rummaging in your coat pocket for a condom. i undid my bra, took off my panties, sat cross-legged on the bed.

you walked back in, the foil packet glinting in the moonlight. bands of bluish-white streaked across the room, across us.

hi, i said, tucking my hair behind my ear.

hi, you replied, matching my smile.

you really can get high off the sensation of someone's skin against yours.

17. live más?

i was distracted all day at the studio, singing off-key and missing cues.

jake threw up a hand to stop me, walked into the soundbooth.

evan, what the hell? you're off, he barked.

i know, i know, i groaned. *i've just been... having some problems at home. i'm distracted.*

well, get undistracted. we've got a month. we gotta lay this down.

i know, jake. contrary to popular belief, i'm not stupid.

just... take a lunch break, and get your shit together. i could be making a lot more money right now.

i rolled my eyes and put down my guitar. the rest of the band timidly walked in.

yo, evan, everything all right with the lady? my bass player asked.

it's nothing. i scrolled through the list of nearby restaurants on my phone. *anyone up for burritos?*

my drummer, a skinny little brat who's a little bit too fond of speed, crossed his arms over his chest, knee bouncing up and down.

hey, man, tell us. your girlfriend okay?

seriously, it's nothing. she's just been kinda sick lately. a stomach bug or something.

i could tell no one really bought it, but after a few steak burritos, we were tighter, and actually got a considerable amount done.

skyler, the audio mixer, approached me at the end of the day as i was packing up my guitar.

hey, evan, she said, pulling her long, lavender-dyed hair into a ponytail, eyebrow ring glinting in the light from the floor lamps. *good work today.*

oh, hi, skyler, i replied. *thanks.*

heard your girlfriend hasn't been feeling well, she said.

yeah, she's just been kinda —

my phone dinged. i pulled it out of my pocket, saw it was a text from you. biting my lip, i opened it. all it said was *the test was right.* i didn't even really know what to feel. an uncontrolled sound of surprise left my lips.

what is it? skyler asked.

i looked to her, shrugged, and said,

my girlfriend's pregnant.

18. sweet relish.

we woke up naked, tangled in the sheets, still smiling in the afterglow. you ran a hand down my arm, kissed my cheek.

good morning, you whispered. i rolled onto my back.

good morning yourself, i replied. *you want breakfast? i think we've got eggs.*

almost lunchtime, actually. it's nearly eleven, don't you have to get to work?

i had never slept this late, not even when i was hung over. but i felt deliriously drunk.

actually, i countered, smiling, *i think today will be my day off.*

well then. you wanna go out?

where? i asked, staring up at your brown eyes.

i dunno, superdawg sound good?

and there we were, sitting at the cramped counter of superdawg, huddling together for warmth. i gave you my pickle (i've never liked them), so i got half your fries in return. even long after we had finished our food, we kept talking, about anything we could think of — the upcoming election, the last books we had read, each other's tattoos and piercings. you wanted to know how long my nipple ring had been there, i wanted to know more about the words on your shoulder.

nunca parar, you said. *it means 'never stop' in portuguese.*

portuguese?

my dad was brazilian. he and my mom were flight attendants.

that's cool. did you get the little plastic wings and shit?

you laughed.

oh, yeah. all the time.

so your dad was an immigrant?

you nodded.

he came to america when he was fifteen, with his older brother, my uncle manoel. eventually my dad found his calling. and his wife. they were both based out of philly. their first kiss was when their plane was grounded during a snowstorm.

aww, i cooed. *that's so sweet. were they away a lot?*

you shook your head, pushing your glasses further up the bridge of your nose.

nah. my mom took time off for a while after she had my sister. but my dad was an old pro at philly to orlando. bought me disney shit in the airport all the time.

and he taught you portuguese.

a bit. i've attempted some duolingo to learn more, but it hasn't been too successful.

does your sister speak some too?

she actually doesn't speak much of anything, you said, tripping over your words.

hmm?

you paused, drawing your straw through your vanilla shake. you had ordered coffee earlier—black with five sugars. i couldn't even imagine two.

my sister was in the accident. she was just hurt. like, a lot. she's in a wheelchair; she still lives with my aunt and uncle out in jersey.

oh my god, i said, eyes wide. *so she can't speak?*

no, she can, just not a lot. she has a nurse who helps her write emails, so we keep in touch that way.

what's her name?

melissa.

i'm an only child. i always wanted a sibling.

you shrugged.

it's fun sometimes. a pain most of the time.

i'm sure she's sweet.

it's rough, sometimes, being away from her.

i took a final sip of my soda.

so, i asked, *we have a plan for today?*

you smiled, and i suppose we knew.

i don't think we stopped holding hands all day.

19. the mistake, part two.

when i came home, you were sitting in the backyard, under the avocado tree, knees pulled into your chest, feet bare. some sort of sprite, dirt under your toenails and hair blowing in the warm breeze. i'm still so disturbed by summer in winter.

hey, i said from the doorway. dead leaves were scattered on the patio. you looked up, wiped your eyes with the heel of your hand.

hey.

i walked across the yard, the ground giving under my sneakers. i sat down, cross-legged, in front of you. reached out and touched a curl of fire.

everything's gonna be fine, i whispered. *we have enough money.*

your album hasn't even been released yet, you replied, looking down, spinning a gingko leaf in your fingers. it had blown over from the neighbor's yard.

we can turn the second bedroom into a nursery. clear out all my music and whatever.

you sighed.

you don't even understand. there was a strange spite to your voice, tiny shards of ice. *if i get rid of it, my dad will call me a godless murderer, if i keep it, my mother'll call me a slut, and —*

shh. it doesn't matter what they think. you know it doesn't.

i know, you replied, playing connect-the-dots with the freckles on your knees. *i just —*

evan.

what?

i have something for you.

yeah?

i reached into my pocket.

i suppose for now it's just a placeholder, you could… trade in it later, I guess.

what the hell are you doing?

i pulled out the ring i got at a cheap jewelry store on my walk from the bus stop. silver with a small, rough blue stone in the middle. never had you struck me as a diamond type of girl. you just smiled, tears in your eyes.

evan lydia, will you marry me?

you nodded furiously, letting your tears fall, holding out your left hand. i slid the ring onto your finger — somehow it fit perfectly, by chance — and held you close.

i put a hand on your stomach, as if i could really feel anything. just knowing there was something, really.

skyler brought in doughnuts and everyone called me a dad-to-be and it was a little scary and we laid down four tracks perfectly and then my manager told me i'm going on a solo tour for the entire summer.

i really need to get better at saying no to people.

20. hold the guac.

i guess, after that, we were addicted. my roommate came home from colorado to find us sitting on the couch playing video games and drinking yoohoo.

um, evan, who the hell is this?

evan, i replied. *my boyfriend.*

that was the first time the word had been said aloud, but i liked the way it rolled off my tongue. you didn't fight it, and the sex stayed good. you were still couch-hopping, worried about being forced to go back to the shelter. but by easter, becca had moved in with that guy. (marshall, i wanna say? whatever, they broke up soon enough and she moved to new orleans.)

i took you out to dinner (tacos, because the thought of shawarma made me want to puke) and made my proposal. the things feminism has made it okay to do. marlo thomas meant well, going braless and all, but come on.

you accepted, squeezing my hand across the table, ignoring the salsa stain on my top.

and i'm not just saying yes because i need a place to sleep, you assured me, not wanting to talk about that sublet. *i would say yes no matter what my situation was.*

yeah? i felt myself blushing. storm drains gurgled with still-melting snow.

i love you, evan.

yup, we were doomed.

21. baby-proofing.

we didn't really know what to do. we threw out the alcohol, and i agreed to stop drinking while you were pregnant (even though i hadn't touched a drop since the illegal rum that got us into this mess in the first place.)

we started cleaning out what was technically the second bedroom. but we had yet to tell anyone outside of our closest friends. you bought prenatal vitamins and nervously followed mommy instagrammers, dreading elastic-waist jeans.

you hadn't told your boss yet, or anyone you worked with.

as you walk out the door, i can see your ankles starting to swell above your white canvas shoes, and i worry. it keeps me entertained, somehow.

22. ball four.

you took me to a cubs game. i didn't really understand baseball, but you were a good teacher. you bought a round of hot dogs and beers and explained walks and errors and how to keep score. the kiss cam never found us, but you held me close on the train home.

my parents now knew i had a boyfriend, that i was living with someone.

every day, they asked about you, and every day, i felt my mouth turn coppery, as though i was about to vomit.

23. blood and water.

during lunch, i figured out what time it was in new jersey and called my aunt and uncle. he'd be at work, of course, but aunt leonor was practically borderline agoraphobic. she picked up on one ring.

evan! she exclaimed. *how are you? how's the album coming?*

good. it comes out in april, i told her.

and we'll be getting copies?

yeah, of course. i didn't even know if it was coming out on cd but i guess i could figure out how to burn them. *make sure melissa gets one.*

she will, don't worry. how is everything? how's lydia?

it was easier for them, honestly. you didn't seem to mind that much.

she's, um… well, actually, she's expecting. we're expecting.

i held my breath, waiting for catholic hellfire, but it never came.

oh, that's so wonderful! she shrieked. *congratulations, when is she due?*

september. we're, um… we're engaged, too. i'll fly everyone out here for the wedding, don't worry.

evan, i wouldn't miss it for the world.

leonor and manoel always wanted to have kids. they had been trying for years, and had been considering a surrogate until the crash. i guess they saw us as a blessing, even though we were both way beyond the cute-baby stage and my sister was, to put it plainly, drooling into a cup.

and now they'll have a sort-of grandchild (grand-niece? grand-nephew? are you going to be their niece-in-law?) to obsess over and i'm sort of thankful we're three thousand miles apart, actually.

24. the backs of our brains.

we settled into a sort of routine as the spring turned into summer.

i would wake before you, as i had to leave for work earlier. i guess everyone buys shawarma before buying vinyl records . i would make coffee and heat up frozen waffles. real maple syrup was one of our few investments, back in those days.

you would take the first shower, wandering into the kitchen and mumbling *good morning,* still shuffling through a half-sleeping state.

we would eat our waffles and drink our coffee and share the newspaper. you always did the sudoku. you never asked me if i wanted to do it. i did.

i would put on my uniform, fitting my name tag into the familiar pinholes on my blouse. you were always still in your pajamas when i kissed you goodbye.

i would suffer through long, boring shifts, missing you as though you'd been gone for years. at lunch you'd send me an email of the lyrics you'd dreamed up while stuck behind the counter. i'd spend the afternoon humming.

i would come home to you strumming your guitar, figuring out the chorus. i'd open a window wide and work on my forever-unfinished paintings.

we'd cook dinner together, if boiling water for ramen really counted as cooking, and we'd eat while watching tv, cuddling in our sweatpants and fuzzy socks. we'd rarely go out. i think we saw maybe two movies that summer. i guess we liked it that way.

we'd lay in bed, on our backs, holding hands, staring at the ceiling until we both fell asleep.

i hadn't been an insomniac until you moved in. but it seemed like a blessing.

25. save the date.

we finished laying down the album today, a week before pressing was supposed to start. cutting it close, but it'll come out when it's supposed to. i was just glad that i didn't have to deal with these lame freelance musicians anymore. i'm better when it's just me and a guitar, but record labels are in the business of fucking me senseless.

my agent was waiting for me as i walked out of the studio.

hello, evan, he said. *coffee?*

he held out a starbucks cup. i gritted my teeth and took a sip. of course he didn't put in enough sugar.

neil, we need to talk.

no shit we need to talk, he replied. *you still haven't confirmed you're doing this tour, and I need to book the hotels and flights, like, tomorrow.*

i contemplated spitting on his snakeskin boots.

i don't wanna do it, i replied, dropping my barely-drank coffee into the wastebasket at the end of the hallway.

what? he said it with disgust, like a popular girl turned down for the prom.

i can't do the tour. my girlfriend's pregnant.

i keep forgetting to say *fiancée*. whoops.

pregnant? funny, didn't think you had it in you.

funny, i thought you were an adult, i snapped. *this is why you should never do business with someone younger than you.*

i'm joking. lighten up, for god's sake. when's she due?

september.

the tour ends in august. you'll be home in plenty of time.

but what if she goes on bed rest or something goes wrong —

calm down, jesus. she seems like a pretty self-sufficient lady.

her family lives in wisconsin, it's not like they can help out. and we're getting married in may.

you sent out email invites last night. other couples have fancy paper and shiny inks. other couples have designer gowns and cakes from bakeries they show on tv. we've got a justice of the peace booked, and that's about it.

what day?

the twelfth.

okay, fine, but after that, you're touring. make the honeymoon short. and don't forget, the europe tour starts in december.

i rolled my eyes.

let's not act like this is getting big.

i don't want you talking like that, neil said, pointing in a scornful-parent way. *that's some quality music you're laying down there. you've got the ep on spotify, y'know, it's doing well. just gotta hope for one of those tiktok kids to get into it.*

how much did your boss pay you to say that? i asked, walking out of the studio, not waiting for him to call after me.

i'm sick of everyone but you.

26. exponential decay.

we took a greyhound to wisconsin over fourth of july weekend, to (gulp) meet my parents. it's hard knowing you'll lose every argument you enter. you sat next to the window, fascinated by the cows and the pastures, as if you had never seen anything like it before.

i pulled my knees to my chest and figured that, if i didn't *think* about throwing up, i *wouldn't*.

they greeted us at the bus station, my mother in a frozen botox smile and my father in horn-rimmed glasses.

mom, dad, this is evan.

even though i had prepared them for it, they laughed. and hugged you. i winced, but you took it in stride.

he's so handsome, my mother gushed. i excused myself to go buy dramamine, although i wasn't sure if it really worked after you got off the bus. time to find out for sure.

my mother made corned beef (*it's july*, i moaned. *it's part of our heritage*, she replied. as if you're unfamiliar with irish culture, they dye the fucking rivers green) and cleo, that old bitch, sat on your lap all through the meal, kneading your thigh.

i've always loved cats, you said, petting her gently. *i'd like to get one someday.*

our building doesn't allow pets, i said, terse.

pshaw. the guy across the hall has like, six rabbits.

rabbits are different.

not really.

my parents' gazes ping-ponged from me to you, forks suspended above their bowls. his voice cracking from the tension, my father announced:

there are fireworks at ten! you two lovebirds want the house to yourself?

daddy, i said through clenched teeth.

we'll go to the fireworks, you said. *she's just tired. needs some coffee.*

i love being talked about as though i'm not in the room. as though i'm the *pet* that's not in the room. liddle shweepy evan, don't say a word.

i was only half-done when i said i was going upstairs. no one fought it. i curled up on my bed, the bed i spent the first eighteen years of my life in, while you laughed at one of my father's lame jokes. i suppose you've always been better at going through the motions.

later, you walked in, sat on the edge of the mattress. my makeup had started rubbing off on my pillowcase.

are you okay?

i released a long breath.

they make me anxious. and i knew they were going to like you, but instead they love you, and that actually just makes everything worse and —

shh. don't ever be embarrassed of where you came from. ever.

there was an honesty in your eyes i couldn't argue with. you kissed my forehead.

i love you, i whispered.

you held up your hand, that little half-smile on your face.

pinky swear?

i locked my finger with yours, looking up at you through my bangs.

pinky swear, darling, that we won't let this destroy itself.

27. the stars aren't falling.

with your friends from work, you went shopping for wedding things. shoes? a veil? what do you even still need, now that you've got the overpriced dress you'll never wear again? not that i know you bought it. not that i found it in our closet.

the last time i had been in a suit was my senior prom, and god, i hated it. or maybe i hated the girl. i just wanted a hand to hold. isn't that what we all want, really?

this doesn't feel much different from senior prom, and i know that's a problem, but to be honest, but i don't care about making this some bridal magazine fairytale. i don't care if you're in sweatpants and flip-flops, hon. i just want to marry you. i just want to hold our baby. i just want to be together.

and i just want this numbness to go away.

28. your new best friends.

my parents couldn't get enough of you. they kept asking about new jersey as if it were a foreign country, wanting to know about the beaches and the governor and what you thought of hooligans on some reality tv show.

you brought a copy of the poster i drew for your upcoming show.

oh honey, it's beautiful, my mother gushed. *you really should do more of this. you're wearing yourself too thin at that restaurant.*

like she knows a goddamn thing.

i have to put money on the table somehow.

you should enter one of those art shows, my father suggested.

dad, i moaned. he sighed, looked to you.

she's never believed in her own talent.

i volunteered to buy dinner. i drove to the supermarket, bought pork chops, and cried in the produce section. because i knew. i knew when they said *she's never believed in her own talent,* they really meant *we wasted a lot of money on art school.*

this entire thing was a mistake.

29. what to expect.

on your day off, maybe the first one you've had in a year, we went to the doctor for an ultrasound. four months already. i was fascinated by your transformation. you fretted over stretch marks, rubbing creams on your skin, but i found the thin white tracery beautiful. decorations.

you sat on the exam table, shivering.

you cold? i asked.

a little. the ac's too high.

here. i took off my hoodie, draped it over your shoulders. *better?*

you nodded. i kissed your cheek.

the technician came in, glancing at a clipboard.

miss zahner?

you raised your hand a bit.

that's me.

well, if you could lift your shirt up for me, and then we'll be all ready to start. how far along are you?

thirteen weeks.

wonderful.

you lifted your t-shirt, gently touching the pale skin. i grasped your hand and kissed your fingers. the technician sat down.

any issues so far? morning sickness?

just a little, you replied. *some weird cravings. but mostly i've been focusing on our wedding.* we looked at each other, smiling. *we're getting married next month.*

congratulations. the technician glanced towards me. *you're the father?*

um, yeah. i didn't know it was being doubted.

she went through the routine, squirting the gel on your stomach, applying the probe to your skin. holding your hand, we looked up at the monitor, at the tiny person inside you. tiny hands and feet and legs and arms.

there's the face, the technician said, pointing to the screen.

oh my god, i said, amazement in my voice. *oh my god, honey.*

you laughed a bit.

i thought i was gonna cry way before you did, babe.

i gave you a stinkeye, jokingly.

would you like to know the sex? the technician asked.

with a deep sigh, we answered *sure,* in unison.

a girl, she said. *and a very healthy-looking one.*

we exhaled together, as if we had both secretly been hoping. i'm still a mess of shock and panic and surprise and disbelief. i'm going to be a father. i'm going to have a daughter. we're going to have a daughter.

no dating until she's sixteen, i whispered on our bus ride home. you put your head on my shoulder.

our daughter, you said.

now you're sitting on the bed, eating ice cream and organizing your paints, laptop open both to baby-naming sites and bridal planning sites.

everything seems premature. your name lists, your nursery-decor plans, our excitement.

30. page-turning.

by mid-august, kids were buying school supplies and we were all fucking sick of summer. but still you tried to squeeze out the last few drops, buying popsicles and coming to the shawarma restaurant in the middle of the day, convincing me to fake an illness and go to the navy pier with you.

and unfortunately, i said yes every time. i told my boss i had a dentist appointment or had to pick someone up from the airport or had a migraine. it went on, even as the first of the leaves changed. you were like a drug, and part of me hated you for that.

by october, i was asked to leave. they needed someone more reliable, they told me.

you came home to find me blasting sad music and painting formless florals in my pajamas and biting my lip so hard it was starting to bleed.

i told you about it. you pulled me into a hug, kissing my forehead.

everything's gonna be fine, baby, i promise.

i didn't want to be anyone's *baby*. i just wanted to do something right.

31. pits.

a post went up on my website about the summer tour. shows in the big cities sold out, sickeningly. you stood behind me, peering over my shoulder at the computer screen.

look at this, sweetie, you said softly, running your fingers through my hair. *look at all these people who want to see you.*

i don't want to do this. like, at all.

it's only for a little while. you'll be back when i give birth to madison.

that's really what you're thinking? i asked, grimacing.

what's wrong with it?

um, everything.

you pursed your lips, walked towards the kitchen window.

jesus h. christ, you sighed. *we're never gonna get a single avocado on that tree.*

i looked towards you, ginger hair aglow in the late-afternoon sunlight, and back towards the computer screen. last ticket gone for the boston show.

maybe we will, someday.

32. crunchy brown leaves.

finding another job wasn't that hard, actually, and it worked out better than i thought it would — one of those expensive tourist steakhouses was hiring. i had to wear a button-down blouse (they'll never work on anything bigger than a b cup, let's be honest) and fancy shoes, but i got to sleep in.

good morning, you'd whisper, every morning. i would kiss you, every morning, and let my hands travel to the edge of your boxers. there was something so joyful, knowing i could make you *feel*.

on sunnier days, we'd go to millennium park and sit on a bench. you'd bring your guitar, tune up, and start playing for strangers. covers of trashy pop songs, classics. a few original pieces, when the crowds were thinner. i was your groupie, in awe of every note.

there was something about your smile, your songs, that transcended time. your exhales were my inhales. we saw with the same eyes.

at home, you'd play the songs that were only for me. i was *lydia* in those lyrics, but i liked it.

one night, as we were falling asleep, you said,

i should really record a demo,

and my heart stopped.

33. maybe it's the msg.

i keep having these falling dreams. i wake up right before i hit the ground, startled, unsure of where i am. another one last night.

i think the comforter's too thick, i was coated in sweat when i woke up. i really need to stop drinking so much beer.

i turned over, saw that you were still fast asleep, and part of me hated you a little bit.

as i sat up in bed, rubbing my temples, you stirred and opened your eyes.

evan? you mumbled, voice thick with sleep.

yeah, babe?

can you bring me a glass of milk?

sure. i leaned down, kissed your cheek. a bit of the pounding in my head went away. *do you want it warmed up?*

yeah.

i went downstairs, poured milk into a saucepan, watched the coils glow orange. i like how everything's a little softer without my glasses. the house in back of us still had all the lights on, music thumping. remember when we went to bed at 3:30?

fionna wove between my legs as i headed back upstairs. her eyes were like moons in the darkness.

i brought the milk to you, and you drank it greedily, as though you had been deliberately starved for months.

she's hungry, you said, wiping your mouth.

you know what name i like? i asked, walking back towards my side of the bed. *annie.*

anna?

no. annie.

it's nice. you didn't seem convinced.

i climbed back into bed, and you rolled onto your side, facing me.

you were awake, you observed, reaching out to stroke my unshaven cheek.

i've been having trouble sleeping. y'know, stress. i was quick to catch myself. *not about the wedding, though. not at all.*

it's about the album, isn't it? you said, in a knowing tone.

i guess. i wasn't sure if i was telling the truth. no one does, when it's two in the morning and you're running on chinese food and irrational fears.

honey, they're gonna love you. you know they will. i can already see the rolling stone headline, you whispered, leaning in close, lips tracing mine. *'evan arinos, acoustic wunderkind.'*

i think you officially lose all chances of being a wunderkind once you turn thirty.

go to sleep, sweetie.

you kissed me goodnight (or good morning, considering it's already tomorrow.) we can't be rough, not anymore. the doctor says we can still have sex, but it's the last thing on either of our minds, at this point. i just want to hold you close, keep you safe. i feel i haven't had enough opportunities for that.

i hugged my knees to my chest, wondering why, feigning sleep next to you every night, i still feel like the loneliest man in the world.

34. the grudge at the foot of the bed.

november thirteenth. your birthday. it was a friday, but we didn't care about superstitions. we all have black cats sitting on our doorsteps.

luck is just what you make of life, you insisted, pouring sugar into your coffee, practically by the cup.

what do you want to do today? i asked. *you pick.*

you sighed, put your chin in your hands.

what's a common twenty-fourth birthday activity?

i shrugged.

i wouldn't know.

you thought a bit more, sipping your coffee.

let's get a cat.

i nearly did a spit take.

what?

i mean, this place is totally big enough for a cat. we can put the litterbox in the second bedroom, and the food can go over there —

that's what you want for your birthday? a cat? i said it with disdain, disgust.

you love cats, you offered.

no i don't.

what about cleo?

that bitch has had it out for me my entire life.

we'll get a nice cat. from a shelter.

i sighed.

fine. we'll get a goddamn cat.

evan, come on, don't get pissy.
i was pouting less after i got out of the shower. we went to the animal shelter a few blocks over, found a gray kitten with a bottle-brush tail and wide yellow eyes, and i suppose we both fell in love. *fionna*, we decided. we cooed over her little paws and little nose and it sickened me, because i had to fall asleep knowing you were right.

35. release.

my aunt, uncle, and sister got a copy of the album. your parents got a copy of the album. my friends, from l.a. and chicago and new jersey, did not get copies, just spotify links.

i got sick of the artwork pretty fast, even though you painted it. a blank outline of a man holding a guitar. me. surrounded by colorful monsters, more cartoonish than scary.

but then i realize that's what the album is about — the demons that have been hiding in the corners of my mind. and it scares me a bit that you're able to read all my racing thoughts.

all the smeared ink, all the sheet music, all the long nights banging my head against the wall just to come up with a chorus — it's all in one product now. it's just noise in headphones.

somehow, it's anticlimactic.

36. truth in advertising.

strawberry syrup and buttermilk on our breaths, we came home, laughing about nothing. i walked towards the bedroom.

there's another part of your present waiting for you, i whispered, sidestepping the cat.

i had spent a good portion of my paycheck on a black lace bra and panties. i wanted a merrywidow, but corsets and the twenty-five pounds i can't get rid of just don't get along.

i emerged from the bedroom, leaning against the threshold, watching your eyes go wide. we're fading into another winter, but somehow our bed still blazes bright.

we found each other in the darkness, lacing fingers and legs and lips, feeling the other ripen. you kissed the hollow of my neck, i dug my nails into your back. i felt you above me, our thighs entwined, and suddenly i didn't care about how fat i felt that day.

everything was skin and sweat. i held you close, smiling over your shoulder as you gasped. your fingers traced my curves as we sighed in unison. so enthralled by each others' existences.

before we fell asleep, you turned to me and said,

i booked a recording studio for next week. ivy said she could get me connected.

connected? i asked, twisting a lock of hair around my finger.

like, an agent. a record company.

this is what you want?

of course it's what i want. this is all i've ever wanted.

i believed you.

stupid girl.

37. arrival gate.

three days until the wedding. you have that glow everyone always talks about. my blushing bride.

we went to pick up my aunt, uncle, and sister from the airport. leonor kept gushing about how healthy you looked. *healthy.*

can i touch your belly? she asked.

of course, you replied. *jesus, strangers at the supermarket want to touch it. they think it's good luck or something.*

leonor placed a hand on your stomach, smiling.

oh my goodness, she whispered. *she kicked.*

the two of you smiled together, and manoel pat me firmly on the back.

you must be so excited, he said. all i could do was nod.

melissa was in her wheelchair, hands in her lap. i hugged her tightly, asked how she was.

happy, was all she said. the flight attendant pushed her along as we went to baggage claim. leonor asked about morning sickness.

oh no, i'm past that, you chirped. *now i'm just pissing like a racehorse.*

suddenly, you turned pale, glancing towards my sister. melissa's older than me, but she just doesn't seem like someone you can curse in front of.

are you still working? manoel asked.

yup. at the diner.

i've been trying to get her to stop, i defended.

i'm only five months. he gets worried over nothing.

the blood boiled in my veins. the ob-gyn told you to take it easy. double-shifts at a greasy spoon—in goddamned south central, to boot—that's not taking it easy.

but what i think doesn't matter. i'm just supposed to tell you that you don't look fat and buy you pickles and rub your feet and not yell at you.

rolling stone called my album *weak*.
38. commitment-shy.

you kept playing shows, making lists of songs to record. none of them were *lydia* songs. none of them were *my* songs.

i think they'll like it, you said, fingertips on the frets.

of course they will, i replied, kneeling behind you and kissing your cheek.

you can paint the album cover.

mhmm. i twirled a strand of hair around my finger.

are you mad about this?

i looked to you.

no. no, no, not at all. i'm proud of you. i support you, entirely, you know that.

okay. i just… i don't know, i worry.

about what?

you sighed, ran your fingers back through your hair.

evan, i might have to move, if i get a record deal. new york, or los angeles, and i mean, long-distance would be really hard, and i love you, i'd want to make it work —

shh. i placed a finger on your lip. *i'll go wherever you do. you know i will.*

there was some sort of earthquake in my soul, and i knew: we were in this, for the long run, and it was terrifying.

39. i'm borrowed, you're blue.

melissa watched me adjust my tie, standing in front of the hallway mirror.

handsome, she said.

she looked beautiful, in a soft blue dress, a white sweater covering her mangled, twisted limbs. her dark curly hair was pulled up, a strand falling in her eyes. she looked like our mom. kind and wise and beautiful.

before our parents met, my mother was in the running to be miss new jersey. she was always the winner in my father's eyes. their wedding portrait hung on the wall next to leonor and manoel's. i don't know how they can stand that, being haunted.

i pushed melissa out the door, waited for you under the avocado tree. your parents were in the front row, holding hands, crying already. my backers from the recording sessions were there. ivy had come all the way from chicago. she waved and gave me a thumbs-up. i bit my lip, let out a nervous breath.

everything melted away when i saw you. emerging from the house, in a long, strapless ivory dress, your hair gently curled and tumbling to your back, brushing against your pale, freckled shoulders. carrying a bouquet of purple irises.

my princess.

i held your hand, under the avocado tree that will never bear a fruit. we recited our vows (*i, evan, take you, evan*—giggles abound) and slid the slim silver rings onto our fingers. you'll have to get yours resized when the baby comes.

the justice of the peace told us to kiss, and we did, to applause, tears in our eyes.

you're mine. i'm yours. before we pulled apart, i felt your pinky lock with mine.

i hugged you tight, arm around your back, burying my face in your shoulder.

fuck 'em all. we're happy here. here, under this tree, in this house, in this city.

believe me, darling, please.

40. with a k.

i hate tourists. it still baffles me that they come to *chicago*, of all places. i didn't understand what people came to see. the cubs? navy pier? the hot dogs? it's not terribly unique. it didn't have the prestige of new york or the glitter of los angeles. no one went to chicago to get famous.

the tourists glare at me on busy nights, as though i'm personally responsible for their hunger. i hate them, just a little, drinking wine that costs more than our rent and eating steaks shipped from south america, as if the way it's cut really makes it worth more.

the other servers know what it's like. the nights when you make just pocket change in tips. the nights when nothing's cooked right and suddenly it's your problem. the nights when you're allowed a two-minute cry in the break room before heading back out to face the people who fundamentally hate you, because you're never fast enough for them.

those are the nights when i come home to you, and you hug me, without even knowing what shit i've gone through, and we slow-dance for nine minutes and thirty-seven seconds to a sad song that was released when we were both still in elementary school, before we were allowed to be sad.

41. the airline lost our hearts.

there was something sort of… *breathless* about married life. for a few perfect days, we snuggled together on the couch and felt the baby kick in the kitchen. our rings made little *dings* against our coffee mugs and we switched our statuses online, together, at the same time.

everything was
together.

but now i'm on a plane to seattle for the beginning of the tour. i miss you already, waving goodbye as i walked into security, a hand on your belly.

has anyone hijacked a plane for love? i just want to get the airports shut down for the whole summer so i have no choice but to stay home with you.

42. introductions.

you wanted to introduce me to your aunt and uncle, come to new jersey for christmas.

they've been dying to meet you. you can get time off from work, right?

probably. i'm this close to quitting, anyway.

not now, you warned. *you know we can't afford that.*

well, we'll talk about that later. just tell me the dates and i'll put in a request for a few days off.

i was thinking we'd spend actual christmas here. like, leave on the twenty-sixth and come back on new years'.

sure. i flicked through cosmo's instagram story, crinkling my nose at another sex position only possible for olympic gymnasts.

do you even want to go?

of course i do. i know how important they are to you.

you're... you're gonna meet my sister, too.

okay.

melissa. she's braindead.

not really, i insisted.

more-or-less.

evan, i want to meet your family. and they want to meet me. it doesn't matter what melissa's condition is, i'm sure we'll get along great.

we fell asleep entwined on the couch, your lips against the cold tip of my ear.

it would be the first christmas i didn't spend in wisconsin.

43. fair trade coffee.

seattle is gray. the pavement seems permanently coated in rain. the people dive under hoods and umbrellas, a city of the faceless. despite the lukewarm streaming numbers, the bar last night was pretty packed. i never thought people would be that interested in seeing a chubby italian-brazilian kid play guitar and crack awkward jokes between songs.

actually, that's a lie. we all plan our acceptance speeches in the shower.

tonight i'm playing the university of puget sound. i shouldn't be looking forward to seeing lithe, dewy sorority girls, but i am.

i really need to remember that i'm married.

44. evergreen.

we bought a tree from a grizzled old man on a street corner. we lugged it up six floors, arguing the entire way, but once it was inside, we sighed together and smiled.

all the lights and ornaments were all brand-new, but they were all ours. someday they'd be old dusty things in boxes. everything is, eventually. i put a menorah on the windowsill, promised to make you latkes.

you made hot chocolate and we sat on the couch and you played a song for me. it was called *dizzy*. i smiled and took slow sips and everything was warm, so warm. you reached in the pocket of your jeans and pulled out something. an early christmas present.

it was a picture of us taken over the summer, in wisconsin, in a frame ornament that said *our first christmas together*.

we pinky-swore it wouldn't be our last.

45. living out of backpacks.

portland, or really just seattle lite. hipsters with nose rings and white people with dreadlocks and me, sleeping alone in a dusty motel 6. i don't have roadies. i'm playing bars and college auditoriums and creaky vfw buildings. someone passes me a check, offers me a beer on the house. i usually refuse it—*just seltzer, please*—and i sign some people's t-shirts and ticket stubs pose for a few pictures.

tonight at a portland coffeeshop, a couple approached me, asked me to sign a poster they bought at the door. i did. as i handed it back to them, the guy asked,

your wife doing okay?

huh?

we saw the picture on your twitter, the girl said. *congratulations. she's beautiful.*

thanks. she's back home in l.a.

on the bus back to the motel, i dialed your number, but you didn't pick up. sleeping, of course.

i don't want you constantly saying goodnight to yourself.

46. other people's houses.

we went to o'hare the day after christmas. i was wearing the sweater you gave me, nubby, thick stitches. not itchy. we sat down in economy, packed like sardines, and you wrapped an arm around my shoulders.

excited?

sure.

is anyone ever really excited about going to new jersey?

but it was my first time on a plane. i didn't tell you that, because i really didn't feel like getting babied. i held your hand during takeoff, trying to ignore the weird noise coming from the engine.

we landed in a gray, smoggy afternoon, biting cold, but your family was warm warm warm,

evan! your aunt leonor (*shee-oh-mah-rah*, we practiced on the plane) shrieked, hugging you tight in the middle of baggage claim. *and evan!* she hugged me too tight. there was no need for a real introduction.

jesus, this'll get confusing, your uncle manoel said with the thinnest of accents.

my middle name is lydia, if that makes it easier, i offered. they seemed to agree.

your sister was timid, sitting in her red wheelchair, next to the baggage carousel. we approached her.

hey missy, you said, smiling. she smiled back, crooked and strained, but a smile nonetheless. she was wearing a thick coat and jeans. the skin on her hands was dimpled and pockmarked, as though it had been burned. *this is lydia. my girlfriend.*

i suddenly regretted recommending that, but i knew she had trouble understanding. all for melissa's sake.

she was beautiful, really. dark curly hair and eyes like yours. but her limbs were shrunk, twisted. it's tragic, how she's been broken.

we gathered into your aunt and uncle's minivan, our gloved hands entwined.

glassboro was pine trees and car dealerships and roadside diners and nothing else, really. your bedroom was sparse; most of your belongings had gone to chicago with you. leonor made dinner, something spicy. and i slept, or tried to, next to you, two in a bed made for one, your breath hot against my neck.

it was nice, being so close to you, but i spent the whole night awake, listening to your sister wheeze herself to sleep.

i don't like the honesty here. it's painful.

47. not my weekend.

so what did the doctor say? i asked, waiting for a flight to santa fe.

he's putting me on bed rest, you whined. *i have to stop working.*

internally, i congratulated you for finally admitting that i was right. but on the outside…

is everything okay?

my fluids are low, apparently. or whatever.

okay, babe, i want you to take this seriously. take it easy.

how are you doing? you asked. i could hear you moving, shifting positions in bed. *did denver love you?*

eh, i think they just want to be friends.

you laughed. *mirth.* i keep thinking of the word *mirth.*

i'm sure that's not true. do i have to worry about groupies?

not at all, i replied. *i'm not exactly thrilling the ladies.*

well, now that i look more and more like a beached whale, i guess i know how you feel.

stop it. you're beautiful.

how would you know? you haven't seen me in a month.

we'll facetime once i get to santa fe. i promise.

okay.

final boarding call. i pulled my backpack on, stood up.

i'm about to board. please, listen to the doctor. get some rest.

just for you, you cooed.

just for annie, i corrected.

i'm not sure if i'm sold yet.

well, now you have all the time in the world to think about it. i love you.

i love you too.

i passed the flight attendant my ticket. she scanned it, waved me through.

i feel weightless, and i don't want to. i don't like how i keep taking off my wedding ring.

48. lose ten pounds, i guess.

new year's eve. last year i was milling around an awkward loft party, looking for someone to kiss. now i'm just reliving high school in this boring town, but at least i'll be able to leave in an hour.

we saw a friend of yours at the supermarket. you bro-hugged and patted each other's backs, catching up. you briefly introduced me.

and we found ourselves at his house, red solo cups and fruit-flavored vodka. you got me a cup of punch, said you'd stay with me all night. you have, holding my hand and showing me off to your friends, all the losers who have yet to leave glassboro. for a while, we made out in the corner, ignoring your single friends.

in an hour, it'll be midnight. in an hour, someone will be crying and someone will be in an ambulance and someone will be passed out in the bedroom, limp with drugs, and we'll be here, watching frozen times square revelers on tv, promising each other that this year is going to be better, because *we're* going to be better.

we've gotten good at lying to each other.

49. wrong-distance.

i still get stage fright, embarrassingly enough. tonight i played a vfw outside of san antonio. my heart beat too fast, my breath shortened, and i felt like i was about to puke. but i went on anyway. i know how much it sucks when you've got tickets for something and the act bails on you. so i did it for my fans, i guess. if i can even call them that.

before i fell asleep, we had a skype call. seeing you just made me forget about my aching joints and my sore throat and the fact that i haven't shaved in days. i was drunk on your smile. fionna meowed at the screen and you kissed her twice, once for you and once for me.

we virtually pinky-swore, squinting and trying to line up our fingers on the screen, laughing. your rings shone against your skin, pale from a month inside.

i love you. i hope you know i'm not lying.

50. secret society.

we drove in silence to the cemetery. i didn't know why you were doing this, but i did, at the same time. you rolled melissa up the path. she held two bouquets of flowers in her lap. i followed behind, burying my chin in my coat against the gray cold. in the distance, we heard cars rushing by on the highway.

we came to the graves. buried side-by-side, one headstone. *joachim estevo arinos, maria contadino arinos.* silently, you and melissa placed the flowers on the ground and i stood, hair blowing in the wind, flecked with the snow that was starting to fall, and i felt painfully, disgustingly left out.

51. breach.

well, i officially have my first psycho fan. tonight i played at some little school in ohio, and some girl jumped on stage, a wild look in her pale eyes. she kissed me. only for a second or two before campus security pulled her off and led her out of the room. i was shaken for the rest of the show, unable to crack the same jokes i usually did.

afterwards, someone came up to the merch table, looking concerned.

that was my friend, she said. *i'm sorry, she's been acting really weird lately, i'm afraid she might be using again —*

don't worry about it. here's hoping it's not already gone viral.

i signed her ticket, and that was that. i'll never see any of the people in that audience again. my album might be everything to them, but my show is just a short little blip in their lives.

to me, they're just anonymous faces in my never-ending crowd. you're the only thing that's clear anymore.

my agent called me as i was heading back to the hotel.

maybe we should get you bodyguards, he mused.

i said nothing. i just wanted to sleep.

52. deep-dished.

back in chi-town, as we had been taught to call it by a man who thought he was a disciple. everything was ice storms and loneliness. even as we huddled together near the radiator, i felt alone. everything in your life was music. booking shows, finding connections, hoping for a record deal. i hadn't really painted in months. not that you noticed.

i fell asleep on the sofa while you were playing in oak park. sorry i couldn't make it. when you came back, you kissed my forehead and i opened my eyes.

hey, sleepyhead, you whispered. *sorry i'm so late.*

it's okay, i replied. *there's pizza in the fridge, if you wanna heat it up.*

you did. i nearly tripped over fionna as i walked into the bedroom. fucking cat. fucking *you*, wanting a fucking *cat*.

you came to bed soon afterwards, belly full of my leftovers. you kissed me while i drifted through the strange in-between of the very early morning.

the next morning, leonor called just to say hi. it was strange. i don't know what it's like, really, to have a family that actually cares.

53. notes from logan circle.

philadelphia. last show on the east coast. i guess the south's a little pissed, but let's be honest, i don't have fans down there. all i care about is that i'm almost back to you. a show in san francisco, a show in fresno, a show in sacramento, and a show in l.a. our show. you'll be there, and i'll perform for you, introduce you to the audience.

maybe they'll love you. i'll love you more than i ever have before. you'll be nearly eight months by then, glowing like they always talk about. what they say about absence? it's sure as hell true.

this city is ugly as fuck, to be honest, but i can see this fountain from my hotel room, and i guess i'm sort of happy to see that it's on.

54. epiphanies and epi-pens.

i fucked up. i fucked up so bad and i don't even know what to do.

i've spent three hours hyperventilating and debating whether or not to call you. but what could you say? you've never put anyone in the hospital. you've never done anything accidentally, i'm sure.

i served a tourist family yesterday, and the daughter, preteen and awkward, ordered a steak (well, of course, what the fuck else would she order?). but she was allergic to nuts. yes, nuts, i remember now, through the fog of tears and fury that clouded me for ages.

i've dealt with these sorts of things before. all the time. but the head chef was out (sick? on vacation? who the fuck even *knows*.) and the sous assured me that the steak was fine, that the sides were fine. the family tipped well.

but today i was called to the back, and my boss told me that the girl spent the night in the er, pumped full of steroids because her heart nearly stopped. her parents were going to sue.

i was asked to turn in my uniform. i'll never waitress in this town again.

but maybe two firings in one year should be a wakeup call.

maybe i should starting doing what i went to school for.

55. have you ever counted the stars?

the san francisco sky is a dark shade of blue, so perfect, the golden gate bridge twinkling in the distance. i bought a sausage sandwich at the pier and took a boat to alcatraz. walked around the prison, the huge barred windows and windy corridors and escape routes dug with spoons. it was eerie standing at the peak of the island, staring out at the bay and the marin county hills, draped in mist.

you feel so close, and yet so far, and i swear, from this high-rise hotel room, i can see straight to north hollywood, and i can see straight to you. almost there, my darling. almost there.

56. phosphenes.

you came home to find me on the couch, drinking vodka straight from the bottle. you put your guitar case down, rushed to me.

hey, you said, prying the bottle from my hand, a concerned look in your eyes. *hey. what's wrong?*

some girl i served last night went to the hospital, i blubbered, a mess of snot and tears. *there was something on her plate she was allergic to and —*

how is that your fault?

it's not, i shrieked. *but they fired me anyway. they fired me and i'm not gonna get hired at any restaurant ever —*

shh. i hate when you think it's okay to cut me off. let me have feelings, christ. but i couldn't say no to you holding me close, couldn't say no to the opportunity to cry into your chest, seeing stars behind my lids. *you don't need to be a waitress. you should sell your paintings.*

i pulled away.

who the fuck would even buy them? i sniffled, wiping my eyes.

lots of people. i promise.

funny thing, promises. they're so fragile, and none of us ever bother to really take care of them.

57. do not disturb.

fuck sacramento. everyone here seems so *depressed*, and before, when i was young and stupid, i thought that wasn't possible in california. *everything's golden,* i kept telling myself, amongst the budget fuck-ups and unemployment lines. no one can be depressed when everything's golden, not even me.

i played at a knights of columbus that honestly looked like it could've doubled for a meth lab. a bunch of dazed suburban kids who thought i somehow saved them, that twelve stupid songs on a stupid album told them that they were worth something. what am i even supposed to say to that? i say i love making music, but i'm unsure of everything now.

just thank them, you insisted over the phone. *be gracious for the first time in your life.*

pregnant you is bitchy. but i'm not allowed to say that.

i shifted in bed, examining the hbo listings. nothing good on tonight. is there ever?

how're you feeling? i asked.

fat, you answered. here we go.

come on.

i am. you're gonna see me in the airport and go running in the other direction.

you're beautiful. i'm practically counting down the seconds, babe.

you're sweet. i almost *heard* you blush. *oh hey, guess what?*

what?

i like annie. like, really like it. and i was thinking maria for a middle name? y'know, for your mother.

i bit my lip, tried not to cry.

i love it.

sounds good. i just got the crib. danny from next door is gonna help me put it together.

that's right, pregnant women can't be trusted with screwdrivers, i said. you laughed, and my heart caved in.

i am getting a little unwieldy.

did you get that bank transfer? i asked.

yeah. thanks.

no problem. i collapsed, bedspread against my back, pinching the bridge of my nose, trying to fight another approaching headache. *i miss you. a lot.*

i miss you too, sweetie. but you'll be home soon.

they want me to tour europe in the winter. i'm gonna fight it. i wanna be home, with you and the baby.

the baby. a pause, for a smile i couldn't see. *she just kicked.*

i sighed.

i'll be home next week.

i'll be there. only a few more days. i'll make you a grilled cheese.

i love you, i said, and i meant it.

i love you too, you said, and i wasn't so sure if *you* meant it.

i took a shower just so the person in the next room wouldn't hear me cry.

58. served cold.

i found an armory show in oak park, one cracked sunday out of a hayden poem. i hit up one of my old college friends for a ride. she picked me up outside the apartment, helped me load the crate of paintings into the backseat of her honda. she spent the entire ride gushing about how long it had been, about how different i looked.

it's funny, because she was exactly how i remembered her.

i sold two paintings the whole day, red smudgy squares to an old lady, blue smudgy squares to a couple around our age. i need to stop reading about rothko.

sorry about today, my friend said on the ride back. *i mean, there are a ton of these all over the city, you might have better luck at another.*

i shrugged, looked out the window. it was cold enough to snow, but it wasn't. that's the most unfair kind of weather, honestly.

i didn't go home right away. i went out, got drunk, reeling in the depressing post-grad-ness of it all. i came stumbling home to you, sleepily asking why i didn't call.

see how it feels, babe? see how it feels?

59. prodigal.

when i stepped off the plane, i finally stopped shaking. seemed i had been for months. i nearly ran through the terminal, knowing you were close. i got past security, and there you were. my red-haired queen, my angel in flip-flops and a long dress, a hand on your belly, so much bigger than it had been before i left. our eyes locked, and as sappy and stupid as it was, there were tears in mine. i rushed to you, kissed you deeply.

look at you, i whispered, pushing the hair back from your face. *jesus christ.*

you grabbed my hand, guided it to your stomach.

welcome home. you smiled, kissed me back. *daddy.*

we walked to the car — still i feel guilty for not knowing how to drive, you shouldn't be on the road in your condition — and i noticed my album lying across the center console.

it helped, you said, blushing. *when i got really lonely. she never seemed to respond much, though.*

you skimmed your fingertips across your skin, maternal. i long for the connection you already have.

you been okay? i asked as we pulled out of the parking lot.

the doctor says i have preeclampsia.

what? wait, is that gonna mess up the baby?

no, no. i just have to take it easy. she said i'd probably feel better once you got home. and now you're home.

you reached out, grabbed my hand, but there was something stiff and unnatural about it all. i feel disconnected, as though i've forgotten all about you. the way you waved to our next-door-neighbor makes me want to beat him up.

the nursery's painted, the crib's put together, and i've had no hand in it. you picked out the colors, the decorations, the spinning mobile. your friends from the diner gave you lots of frilly pink baby clothing, and i didn't help you write the thank-you notes. all i can do now is treasure you, re-learn your curves and your idiosyncrasies, try to forget about all the skinny girls who hugged me and took pictures with me and told me to sign their records *with love, evan arinos.*

even fionna's keeping her distance.

60. little bohemia.

you came to the next armory show, eager to help. i rented a van to get us there and back. i've been flirting with the idea of getting a car, but first i'll need to find a job, a *real* job. at least i can't get fired for what's in the food at a grocery store. maybe that'll work.

we set up a table, and i put out the business cards i had ordered off the internet. *paintings by evan lydia zahner.* you smiled, kissed my cheek.

my aunt and uncle want one, they saw the pictures online.

i'll do something custom, i answered, fiddling with my earrings, jumpy. your videos were getting a lot of hits, and i guess a little part of me wanted to beat you. or at least be even. *for free. they're family.*

the *other* other f-word. it made my stomach lurch. suddenly i'm put off by permanence.

more people bought paintings this time. some even gushed, promised they would look for me at the next show. the sculptor across the way shot me a dirty look, thieving his thunder.

on our way through the parking lot, you held my hand as though you were proud of me. but i knew you weren't. buy me all the congratulatory superdawgs you want, i refuse to believe you've ever fooled a soul.

61. scraps.

i woke up early, suddenly eager and restless. i wanted to clean. the living room had become mess, nothing but takeout food containers and parenting magazines. i found a list scribbled on the back of a receipt: *emily, rory, shayna, helena, rachel. arinos or zahner?*

i sighed, tucked it in my pocket. i knew you weren't kidding about maria, but the i-like-annie thing was definitely bullshit.

you came downstairs, hair mussed, the hem of your robe licking your ankles.

baby, what are you doing? you asked sleepily.

just… tidying up. you want breakfast?

later. i'm gonna take a bath, my back's killing me.

i wiped a smudge off my glasses with the corner of my t-shirt, fed fionna.
still no avocados on the tree out back. oh well.

i found a big box in the closet — a still-unassembled stroller.

i googled it. i could've bought a nice laptop for less. you definitely didn't buy it.

i poured myself a bowl of cheerios and went upstairs, leaning against the doorframe while you sat in the tub. selfishly, i don't want you to leave my sight.

what are you looking at? you asked with a smirk.

excited for tonight? i sat on the edge of the tub, gently rubbed your knee.

yeah. i get to hear all the new songs live. i'm stoked, as the kids say, you answered with a giggle. *but i'm meeting a friend for lunch, i have to get ready for that.*

friend? who? i kinda thought you didn't have any, to be honest.

danny. the guy from next door. he invited me over. you can come, if you want.

danny? i asked, skeptical. you rolled your eyes.

oh, come on. nothing happened. he just likes to cook. he's making meatless meatloaf.

then why the fuck is it called meatloaf? i asked, shrill.

evan, stop. he's been really nice and helpful these past few months. and anyway, i think he might be gay.

i reached into my pocket, pulled out the list.

i found this, so don't think you can hide stuff from me.

your eyes widened, and your snatched the paper from my hand, the ink spreading.

jesus christ. this is old. i don't care.

no. you do. and if you feel this compulsory need to lie to me, i suggest you get that out of your system before we have a fucking baby together.

you sighed, exasperated.

evan —

i stood up.

come on, evan. annie arinos? that's bullshit.

at this point, i only feel at home with my fingers against the strings.

62. post-traumatic.

you booked a show at the university of wisconsin. your first *big* show, but no way to get there. you sat on the couch after getting off the phone with ivy (now your de facto agent), fingers absentmindedly touching the frets, soft notes vibrating in the air, mixing with fionna's obnoxiously loud purring. snow was settling outside, jack frost's sucker punch.

i guess i could take a bus. they said they'd have mics there, so i only need to bring my guitar. but fuck, merch. the seven-inch just came in, and the t-shirts you designed. i guess i'll just have to see if ivy can drive me.

i sighed, slammed the wooden spoon down. dinner would have to wait.

jesus fucking christ, will you stop talking to yourself if we just buy a car?

you turned around on the couch, gave me a look, eyebrow arched high over your glasses frames.

a car?

yes. a car.

i can't drive.

you can learn. i'll teach you.

you turned pale, stood up, began pacing.

no. no, i can't. i can't.

i leaned against the counter, rubbed my temples.

evan, you weren't even in the car when it happened. it was thirteen fucking years ago.

it probably wasn't the right thing to say. actually, it definitely wasn't. but i'm getting sick of your defense mechanisms.

you don't get it. you don't get it, evan.

then help me get it, i said, placing a hand on your forearm.

you stepped away, eyes wide with fear.

you wouldn't… no. we can't get a car. something could happen.

honey, they were hit by a drunk driver, it had nothing to do with how they were driving.

they were driving her home from camp in the poconos, you mumbled, wringing your hands. *their caskets were closed at the funeral. they couldn't fix them.*

i took a deep breath.

okay, we'll talk about this later. go lie down. i'll call you when dinner's ready.

you obeyed, slamming the bedroom door behind you. fionna jumped in the air, ran under the couch. i turned on the tv, squeezing the throw pillow tight, imagining it was your head.

63. nice-enough guys finish last.

danny moved in six months ago, but apparently you didn't bother to introduce yourself until i was away. he opened the door with a beaming colgate smile, and i decided within two seconds that i hated him and/or he was up to no good. he has this psychotic collie — finally, i've found the source of my insomnia.

two evans, back in the neighborhood, he said.

hi, danny, you said, smiling too much. *thanks for having us.*

you placed a hand on your belly as you walked inside, holding your skirt in your fist. you didn't have enough for an entirely new maternity wardrobe, so you're cycling between the same three dresses and a pair of leggings with a few of my old t-shirts.

he shook my hand, catching me in the doorway.

danny wheeler, he introduced.

evan arinos.

she's told me a lot about you.

you live alone? i asked.

for the moment. you're a musician, right?

mmhmm. and you…

personal trainer, he answered. i should've known, from the livestrong bracelet. only tools and personal trainers still wear those things.

i walked inside, put off by the leather couches and stainless steel appliances. i like our house, mismatched floor-sample furniture and a threadbare oriental rug we found on the side of the road somewhere.

he offered us protein shakes, claiming they were mango-flavored.

you are eating for two, he reminded you. you shrugged.

sure. can't hurt.

i took a tiny sip. it tasted metallic, sickening.

we sat on the couch, watching daytime tv as we ate. your ankles are so swollen it hurts to stand for too long. i feel horrible, one mistake responsible for all your pain.

i held your hand, kissed your fingers, but you pulled yourself from my grip. danny kept cracking jokes only you laughed at, making me feel like the junior-high dork against the wall at the dance. but i kept seeing the way he was looking at you, and it made me sick. made my blood boil.

you stood up, smoothing your dress, heading to the bathroom without asking where it was. i crossed my arms, tried to take deep breaths.

want to help me with dessert? danny asked. *i'm making fruit salad. oh, unless you're not done.*

he glanced towards my plate. i had only nibbled my meatless meatloaf. i wanted in-n-out.

nah, i'm good. i'll help.

great. you can cut the pineapple. don't you just love pineapple this time of year? great for you, so much vitamin c.

i followed him into the kitchen, wondering how i could make it look like an accident.

as he chopped watermelon and fed his stupid dog a few bits — that's demeaning, honestly — i turned to him and asked,

how much do you make, as a personal trainer?

depends, danny said. *usually starts at two hundred an hour.*

i wolf-whistled.

well, that explains the stroller.

what?

i put the knife down before i lost my temper.

did you fuck my wife?

what?

simple question, bro. i was gone a long time, and you two seem awfully friendly. she knows where your bathroom is.

it's not that hard to find, he defended. *she's just a friend, honestly.*

that's a thousand-dollar stroller you bought her! you really think i wouldn't see the 'from danny' tag on the box?

she just... maybe it was a bit much, but — i would never. i would never sleep with a married woman —

oh, so if we were still just dating, it would've been okay? she's pregnant.

the toilet flushed and i fell silent. you walked back into the kitchen, hand on your belly, and you saw me, chest puffed out, fists clenched.

we left without dessert. fuck fruit salad, anyway.

64. snake oil.

you trembled the entire el ride out to the car dealership. i gripped your hand, kissed your cheek.

it's okay, i whispered. *you're gonna be okay.*

you were cold and clammy, fear in your eyes. you kept fiddling with your glasses, and i wondered how much you could remember. a phone call. your aunt and uncle crying in the next room. your sister in physical therapy.

we wandered the lot, buried in our thick coats, scarves over our faces. winter in chicago drags on forever, it seems.

we'll get an automatic. they're easier to learn on.

you're really gonna teach me?

probably not in time for the wisconsin show, but i'll drive you to that. oh, and i got a driver's manual, there's a graduated license program you'll have to go through. fewer hoops to jump through, though, because you're over twenty-one.

i'm... i'm still not sure.

it's important, evan. i think it'll help you... cope.

sometimes i realize i'm talking like a tv shrink. and dear god, do i need to stop.

we bought a white 1999 honda from a guy who looked like he was running for president, salt-and-pepper hair and a sneaky smile. you sat in the passenger seat, twiddling your thumbs as we drove back home.

i've never seen your mind work this hard.

65. you've probably heard this song before.

you put on your green maxi dress and your slip-on vans (what has the west coast done to us?), curled your hair and put on makeup.

i want to look pretty for you, you said, while i picked through t-shirts, sniffing them to find what was still clean. would a descendents t-shirt look too try-hard?

on the ride over, my guitar in the backseat, you held my hand across the center console and squeezed tight.

i forgive you, you said. i hadn't said sorry yet, and i had no immediate plans to do so. say all you want, danny isn't just a friend.

there were a bunch of skinny, pathetic kids hanging around outside the phoenix, cheering when they saw me. i rolled my eyes, but you grabbed my hand, halted me.

go, you said. *go say hi to your fans.*

i signed some tickets and some cds, took some pictures. thank god this is nearly over. some kid in a steph curry jersey told me i inspired him to start playing guitar. i couldn't come up with anything interesting to say. i just nodded.

the show went okay. the performances on the east coast were better. maybe i'm just tired. or maybe i still feel weird about playing when i know you're looking at me. you were in the wings, hand on your belly, observing. before *orange county,* the song i sort of wrote about you (but then again, that's every song, they're only *sort of* about you), i leaned towards the microphone and said:

this one's for my wife. say hi, lydia.

still, no one else can know. i don't even know if your parents call you *evan* anymore.

you timidly walked out onto the stage, as though it were full of landmines. waved.

i love this girl, i announced, pulling you towards me. i ignored you fighting against my grip. *we've been married three months and i love her to fucking bits.*

you put on a smile, because everyone was clapping and taking pictures and what the fuck else were you supposed to do? you gave me a glare, as if pleading me to stop, but i didn't. i couldn't.

and this is our daughter, i said, touching your middle. *she's due in a few months. we're gonna name her rachel. right, honey?*

i think you should play the song, evan, you hissed.

i did. everyone screamed when i introduced it. *i've never liked this part of town, but hold my hand and we'll send everyone a postcard as we drown.*

late that night, as we walked up to the bedroom in the darkness, you stopped on the stairs, moaned, bent over.

everything alright? i asked.

you looked to me.

just a stomachache.

66. as-is.

okay. now put it into drive. don't forget to press the brake.

yeah, i know, you snapped.

just reminding you.

you pressed the brake, shifted, slowly inched forward. it took a while to find an empty parking lot, but the remote lots at o'hare were barren enough.

okay, left turn, i instructed. *hand over hand.*

you did, but you accelerated too much and slammed on the brake just before hitting a light pole.

fuck, you muttered, knuckles white against the steering wheel.

it's okay. just less gas next time.

can we be done? you asked, eyes pleading behind smudged lenses. *i just… i can't do this, evan. i can't.*

yes you can, i soothed, rubbing your thigh. *you just need more practice. i mean, i was horrible when i was first learning. once i was driving and i veered so far to the right i almost took out a dairy farm's fence! everyone messe—*

stop with the cutesy wisconsin stories, okay? i just wanna go home.

i sighed.

okay. do you wanna stop for dinner?

i'm not hungry, you answered, opening the driver's door and stepping out into the twilight. the city lit up as we drove back in, but somehow, the magic was gone.

in the apartment, fionna meowed hello and rubbed against my legs while i plucked cans of tomato soup from the shelf. you took off your jacket and kicked off your shoes.

oh, i have a show tomorrow night, you told me. *ivy has a new band and their guitarist flaked on them at the last minute.*

do you want me to come? i asked.

you probably wouldn't like it. it's kinda screamy.

that night, lying in bed, you held my hand, and i started to realize that mine didn't fit perfectly in yours anymore.

67. spontaneous.

i woke in the middle of the night to screams.

evan! you shrieked from the bathroom, startling fionna off the bed. *evan!*

i nearly fell out of bed, sheets tangled around my ankles. i reached for my glasses and ran to the bathroom threshold.

what is —

you didn't need to answer. i didn't even need to ask. you were standing in the middle of the bathroom, shaking, pulling on the hem of your oversized packers t-shirt. crimson blood, running down your legs, pooling on the white tiles.

everything went into hyperdrive, and soon i was in the back of an ambulance, holding your hand, wiping away your tears while trying to hide my own.

they ran tests in the emergency room, didn't tell us a thing. somewhere in the panic, i realized we both weren't wearing shoes. you kept moaning, touching your belly, whispering *my baby, my baby.*

the doctor walked in, glancing at a clipboard, and then she looked up at us.

miss zahner?

jesus fuck, it hurts, you moaned, doubling over. i rubbed your shoulder, kissed you, tried to take away the pain.

we're going to be moving you up to maternity, the doctor said.

she's in labor? i asked, smiling.

no, the doctor asked, and our faces fell. *miss zahner, i'm sorry, you're having a miscarriage and you'll have to deliver stillborn.*

finally, you've broke, and finally, i can't fix you.

68. speed limits.

spring, finally. it was sunny, the river lit up at midday. you've completely given up on learning how to drive. every time you went behind the wheel, you started hyperventilating, and i figured it just wasn't worth it. not yet. the illinois driver's manual sits, gathering dust, in a dark corner of our apartment.

i came back from another armory show to find you cooking dinner, a rare sight. i put down my bags, kissed you hello.

hey. what are you making?

beef stir-fry.

i pursed my lips, tilted my head.

is there an anniversary i'm forgetting? you liked to celebrate weird ones, the first time you wrote me a song and the first time we went food shopping together. some call it quirky, i call it annoying.

no, i just wanted to make something nice. don't act like you're not sick of spaghetti every night.

but you make the best spaghetti.

i got wine, too.

well, thanks. you're sweet.

how'd the show go?

good. the pine trees are selling like crazy.

i'm proud of you.

the calluses on your strumming hand seem to be shrinking. work's been slow. you've been slow and i've been fast, and i worry highway hypnosis will overtake me.

you played some shoot-em-up video game on mute (it's not the gunshots i hate, it's the splattering noises) while i checked my email. there was something from the arts director of the irving park branch of the public library.

they want me to do a mural, i told you. *at the branch a few blocks away. the guy who bought that big couch-sized from me? his wife runs arts stuff there. she's interested.*

that's great, babe, you answered. *when do you get started?*

she wants to see me next week. oh. the night of your madison show. i'm not gonna be able to drive you.

that's okay. i'll take the bus.

you're sure? because i can always reschedule.

no. that's more important than my stupid show, anyway.

don't say that. your music is important too.

you paused the game.

i'm gonna go take a shower, you said, standing up.

i'll join you, i purred, grabbing your wrist.

and i did, my hair sticking to your shoulders as i kissed you, turning the water hotter to try and erase the tension from our muscles, our minds, our hearts.

69. induced.

they injected you with something that made you go into labor, dilate and contract like you were supposed to. like you would've a month from now, had everything gone to plan.

you didn't scream at me like in the movies. you didn't scream or howl or shout or curse. you just cried, uncontrollably, for the eight long, long hours you were in labor. the doctors said you were restraining yourself, sucking it back instead of pushing. but who wants to give birth to something that will never know life?

i stood, bewildered, shocked at your near-silence. you wouldn't let me touch you. every time i stepped closer, you swatted the air in my general direction, like when i was young and i tried to talk to my mother when she was on the phone. *mommy's busy, evan.*

as soon as it was out, they wrapped it up and it was handed off. you were put in a wheelchair and taken to recovery. a social worker approached me.

we can recommend funeral homes, she said.

what?

most families feel a service can help with the grieving process.

i've seen baby coffins on tv. i didn't want to see one in person.

no, just… no, we don't want that. where did they take my wife?

in the elevator, i finally allowed myself to cry. i guess i hadn't realized i was going to be a father until it was taken away. they said it might've been stress. i'm going to die blaming myself. i'm never going on tour ever again. i'll go to community college and sell insurance, for all i care. i'd rather be miserable than see you cry like that ever again.

when i reached your room, you were watching the fourth hour of the today show, eating crackers and sipping apple juice, still deadly pale.

evan, i'm so sorry, i said, wiping my nose on my sleeve. *i can call your parents, if you just wanna rest, or… we don't have to tell them. they said you might be here for another night. i can go home and get some clothes, or a book… just tell me what you want.*

i sat on the edge of the bed, held your hand. finally, you let me close. i kissed your knuckles. you kept eating, sipping, perfectly silent.

babe, i said, *i'm so sorry. just say something, please.*

you looked to me.

i want a divorce.

70. now how much would you pay?

we went to a gallery together, where a friend of mine from college was showing her sculptures. you seemed uncomfortable in your slacks and dress shoes, as though you felt uninvited in your own skin. it's okay, i didn't feel great either. wrap dresses aren't flattering once you get to size fourteen.

lindsey ran across the gallery when she saw us, hugging me tight.

oh my god, it's been so long! she gushed. *how are you?*

good, good.

you look, um... you look great.

i knew she was lying. i've put on weight since graduation. but she's still single, so.

thanks. um, lindsey, this is my boyfriend, evan. evan, this is lindsey. we roomed together freshman year.

it's nice to meet you. is that yours, in the middle? you asked, pointing towards a plaster sculpture of... something. she rarely works without getting high.

yeah. i can dock off a couple hundred, if you're interested in it.

i'm not sure we have room for that, i said nervously, not wanting to admit that i thought it was hideous.

i see. either of you want something to drink?

we can get it ourselves, i said, linking my arm in yours. she rushed off to talk to some tall european-looking man.

so when are you gonna be in something like this? you asked, gazing at the huge paintings and the mobile hanging from the gallery's ceiling.

oh, i don't know. i'm not even sure if i want one. the armory shows are more personal. i glanced at the price tag for one of the photographs hanging nearby. *and no fucking way could anything i paint be worth that much.*

fifteen grand? i think so. how much are they paying you for the mural?

eight. maybe they just feel bad because they're telling me what to paint.

and what's that?

some scene with native americans. all the branches of the library are installing pieces that reflect illinois history, or whatever.

you want a drink? you offered.

ugh, yes please.

we got buzzed on champagne. just buzzed. but lindsey was obviously on something, she kept going to the bathroom and coming back with a self-satisfied smirk and crazed, jungle-cat eyes. you were getting another glass when she strode up to me. i was admiring a large splatter painting, and she leaned over and said,

you know, i've heard hydroxycut is very effective.

what?

honey, i think your freshman fifteen has worn out its welcome. he might want to try it too, i think they make a men's formula.

are you high?

evan, i'm just trying to help you. it's hard for a woman in this business. i mean, for men, it's all talent. for women, i mean, no one's gonna wanna buy stuff from you if you're not, y'know, fuckable —

i shouldn't have, really. but i've wanted to slap that bitch for a long time now.

we left before anything got really ugly. lindsey retreated to the bathroom for another hit, another line, another whatever. we went to gino's east and i cried into our pitcher of beer, because why the fuck should anyone have it together at twenty-five?

71. handyman special.

i'm gonna fucking cry. i can't fucking cry.

why? i asked you. *baby, we've been married three months, we can't break up.*

we shouldn't have gotten married. i didn't even wanna get married.

then why did you say yes when i proposed? i asked, bewildered.

because i thought this baby should have a mother and a father! you shrieked. *but if i knew it was going to die and leak out of me then maybe i just would've gotten an abortion and never have even told you!*

babe, please —

maybe i thought it would fix things, you said, pulling your disheveled hair into a ponytail. *and maybe i thought you'd actually be here for the whole fucking pregnancy and actually commit to being a father instead of flying across the country to play to rooms with ten goddamn people in them!*

hon, you're just —

i'm your wife, and still even our closest friends think my name is lydia!

evan, please calm down.

there. there it is, you said with scorn. *god, i should've dumped you back in chicago. but instead i followed you to this piece-of-shit city with no fucking weather and you're all happy and successful even though, i mean, let's be honest, anyone who actually listened to that album downloaded it illegally, and god, i am so fucking sick of this city and your dumb acoustic punk scene and being nearly twenty-eight and still being a waitress. i'm unhappy and you don't even notice!*

evan, i'm sorry. i grabbed your hand but you wrenched yourself from my grip. *i know we've been distant lately. i didn't wanna go on tour. i really had no choice. but i am committed to being a father. you know that. i read what to expect, like, cover-to-cover on the plane.*

that's not what it's about, you answered, taking another solemn sip of juice.

i don't wanna give up. we've been at this for four years, we can get through this.

no we can't. i can't put up with this bullshit anymore. you're like a child. you care more about being a rockstar than caring for your family. i mean, jesus fuck, you can't even drive a car. you forget to feed fionna half the time, i don't know why i thought you'd be a good father.

no one's perfect. i'm gonna get better. we all get better. don't you remember that night when i told you about the contract? we were so happy. i want that back.

we weren't happy. you were happy.

i groaned, rubbed my temples.

you slept with danny! i insisted in exasperation.

this is exactly what i'm talking about, you said. *you're just going around accusing me of shit you know i didn't do, just because you're mad at me. you'd rather i was gone, because you and i both know that i'm completely useless to you. i'm just some fat girl you can use for a grilled cheese sandwich and a halfway-decent fuck, because inside you're some fifteen-year-old completely unwilling to accept the fact that he has any real responsibilities. you're a coward, evan. you wanted to go on tour because you wanted to figure out a way to get out of this.*

no i didn't. you know i didn't. evan, i love you. i love you and this baby and —

well it's too fucking late, because it's dead.

i caved in. i took off my glasses, fogging with tears, and started full-out sobbing.

please give me another chance. i'm so sorry. god, evan, please.

go home. get some sleep.

you want me to come bring you a fresh set of clothes?

no, i want to give you a headstart on finding a divorce lawyer, you fuckwad.

i stood up, put my glasses back on.

you're gonna regret this, evan.

i think i've filled my life's quota on regrets at this point.

the bus driver asked me if someone died. and for the first time in my life, i didn't lie.

my daughter, i said. *can you stop at kittridge and camellia?*

72. your mother warned you.

when i arrived at the public library, there was a man there, setting up paints and a dropcloth. i didn't know there was going to be another painter.

seems i've permanently moved to the dark.

hello?

he turned around. oh no.

you must be evan.

um, yeah. hi. you are...

james. i'm your assistant.

i put down my bag, started rolling up my shirtsleeves.

i didn't know this gig came with an assistant.

i mean, it's a pretty big space, he said, looking up at the blank wall. i had already sketched on the plaster. *but i can mix paints or bring you water or whatever.*

oh. well. thanks. i mean, you can help paint, too, are you trained?

yeah, i graduated cooper union in may.

cooper union, i echoed. and what brought you to chicago?

i wanted to come back home. i grew up in evanston.

i nodded.

i'm from wisconsin. that's important, remember that. where's the primer?

he pointed to a can by the wall.

wisconsin? am i allowed to make cheese jokes?

i giggled.

stick to like, one a day. that's the quota.

he nodded, smiled.

gotcha.

i spent the rest of the day trying not to think about the muscles ripping under his plaid shirt, his chiclet-white teeth, the way he bit his lip before he talked.

i tried to keep thinking of you, but it's getting harder and harder.

73. old clichés.

you came home from the hospital around dinnertime, deadly pale, with a vicodin prescription. i put down my phone, approached you. when i reached out towards you, you slapped my arm away and walked up the stairs.

evan.

don't talk to me!

baby, i don't wanna break up. we can make this work. i'll be better. i promise.

it's not you, it's me, you answered.

i rolled my eyes, followed up the stairs.

oh, don't give me that shit. four years, evan. four goddamn years. we are not getting divorced just because of one shitty thing. it can happen to anyone, evan!

you turned around, looked me right in the eyes. your hair seemed redder against your especially pale skin. my malibu barbie was gone.

it happened because you were gone for so long. because you don't care about this. at all.

evan, please.

shut up. i'm going to wisconsin. i'm gonna stay with my parents. and tell them why they're actually not gonna be grandparents. and you... you can do whatever the fuck you want. but when i come back, we can decide. on the divorce.

baby, i wanna be with you.

well, i've wanted to leave for years, but you're this grown-ass child who can't bear to be on his own for like, two seconds, so maybe, just maybe, if you grow the fuck up, i'll stay with you.

evan —

i need to pack.

you slammed the bedroom door behind you, blasted the angriest cd you could find. i walked outside to the shelter of the avocado tree.

the house in back of us was having a party. light in the trees, laughter in the air. but when i looked up through the branches, all i saw was you, running around the bedroom, maybe cursing, maybe singing, tearing clothes out of the dresser.

the party was starting to wind down when you walked onto the porch. you pulled off your rings.

i'm not gonna throw them at you.

74. politically correct.

james was a big help. he was good enough that i let him do the backgrounds, some of the little babies in papooses.

you were in madison. you took the bus. i stayed home. real work waited for me, real money, a smidgeon of a real chance.

as i added a highlight to a tree trunk, james turned to me and asked,

any plans for tonight?

eh, not really. my boyfriend's in madison, so i think i'm just staying in.

why's he in madison?

he's playing a show at uw. he's a musician.

the painter and the musician. how romantic, he said, as though he was writing a fairytale.

yeah. i guess. it was all i could say. i kept playing with the necklace you gave me for valentine's, some cheap thing that was already starting to tarnish. everything tarnishes. sometimes you just have to learn to look past it.

i didn't know you were with someone.

i don't, like, advertise it. i'm not in high school.

does he get jealous? he asked.

what?

well, like, if we went out for dinner together after this, would he get mad?

i thought of you, riding the bus to madison, guitar case tucked between your legs, waiting for me to respond to the twelve texts you've sent me, and in the back of my mind, *he doesn't need to know* throbbed like a heartbeat. i shrugged.

sure, why not?

he smiled.

i don't deserve even a shred of happiness. i hope they paint over this mural.

75. the barrens.

i probably should've told my aunt and uncle that i was coming. but i couldn't. once you left, everything became a haze. i packed my bags and sent three months' rent to the landlord and booked a flight to philadelphia. i put fionna in her carrier, paid the fee for her to fly. it's telling, that you didn't even think of bringing her with you. you were so determined to hate every part of me in your life. i left the rings, yours and mine, on the dresser, a reminder of my own stupidity.

a very old woman sat next to me on the plane. she was trying to start a conversation, but i wouldn't let her. my head against the cool plastic of the window, i tried to think if i had spoken to anyone since you left. i hadn't. not even a *good morning* to the guy at the corner shop. i've been drowning in myself these past few weeks, and i didn't know if i even wanted to come up for air.

i took the septa, switched to an nj transit bus, and finally, moon high in the late-summer sky, i arrived at my aunt and uncle's door. there was a strange whistling in the pines, maybe the wind, maybe the devil that populated campfire stories and nightmares.

my aunt answered the door.

i just cried.

76. bomb shelter.

we didn't sleep together. god, you really do assume the worst.

really, all he did was take me to some hole-in-the-wall italian restaurant and we ate a lot of breadsticks. there wasn't any sex. i promise.

when i woke up the next morning, you were just coming in the door, frazzled from a long ride home. you collapsed in bed next to me. i rolled over and kissed you hello.

how'd it go?

great, you said with an almost orgasmic smile. *i really think i should record a full-length.*

that's a great idea. was it? i just want to make rent.

fionna hopped onto the bed, purring, and she promptly sat on your feet. you wrapped your arms around me and gave me this end-of-the-world kiss, and i guess i felt safe with you, maybe for the first time since that first night you spent here.

holy shit, it's really been a year.

77. trust issues.

aunt leonor made me rice and beans, in her pajamas. uncle manoel came downstairs, muttered *que porra é essa?* and went back upstairs.

(*what the fuck is this*, if you really wanted to know. it *was* past midnight, and i wasn't exactly announced.)

fionna peed on the carpet (i promised to clean it up in the morning) and curled up on the couch. my aunt handed me a steaming hot bowl, and i ate greedily, starved on nothing but airplane pretzels.

she sat down next to me, placed a hand on my cheek and kissed my forehead.

meu filho, she whispered, because i guess i've been around long enough to be her son. *everything will be okay. she loves you and she knows it.*

i imagined you back in eau claire, listening to your mother telling you that it happens more often than you'd think, that i was the best thing that ever happened to you.

but that's the thing. i *wasn't*.

she made my bed while i lugged my suitcase upstairs. my room appeared exactly the same, even nine years after leaving home. still the little league trophies and the poster of the brazilian soccer team and the pages torn out of the sports illustrated swimsuit issue, back when i was nothing but unrealistic expectations.

but something felt wrong. i looked across the hall, to melissa's room. there was nothing on the walls, and the mattress was bare. my heart started to pound.

where's melissa?

hmm?

why is melissa's room empty? i asked, voice rising, not caring if i was waking my uncle.

oh, anjinho, she whispered, hugging me tight. *we brought her to a home.*

78. vicariously.

you came to visit me when i was painting. james and i were pretty efficient, and by that point, we were really just working on finishing touches. his hand kept brushing up against mine, maybe on purpose. goddammit.

you held out a coffee from the shop around the corner. i smiled and took it.

thanks, babe, i said. you were wearing your lighter jacket, but you were shivering. march is such a tease.

it looks great, you said, looking up and putting an arm around my shoulders. james stood timidly in the corner, afraid to even introduce himself.

i'm glad you like it.

the head librarian came over, clapped her hands together in joy.

oh, it looks beautiful, she said. *so beautiful.*

thank you, i said with a blush. you smiled like a proud parent. or at least like a parent who was actually proud of me and didn't still complain about tuition prices post-graduation.

there's going to be a gala at the main branch on the fifteenth, she said. *all the artists are invited. we just want to celebrate all these great works and the refurbishments to the library. i hope you'll come.*

i wouldn't miss it for the world. even though there was a ninety-nine-percent chance i'd rather be in sweatpants.

great. and we're looking for some entertainment, like music and stuff, so if you know anyone, let us know.

you lit up like a fucking christmas tree, delighted at the prospect of whoring yourself out.

i can do something. evan arinos, i'm her boyfriend.

oh, the head librarian said, shaking your hand. *sure. just, um… we'll be in touch.*

she walked away, and i crossed my arms.

what? you asked. i rolled my eyes. *no seriously, evan, what?*

79. never plugged in at all.

it's one in the morning, do we have to have this conversation now? my uncle asked from the bed, rubbing his eyes against the lamplight.

yes, we have to have this goddamned conversation now, i said. *why did you send her away? why did you do it without telling me?*

honey, she wanted to leave, leonor said. *she was lonely here. she wanted to see people her own age.*

that's bullshit. you can't just drop her in a home and pretend she's not in your life anymore!

jesucristo, manoel muttered. *go back to california and get a real job!*

manoel, leonor scolded. *you build swimming pools for rich people, you're not one to talk.*

he mumbled in response, turned over in bed. she turned to me, resting a palm on my cheek.

oh anjinho, she cooed again. *we visit her once a week. she's happy there. she really is.*

you should've fucking told me! i wrestled from her grip, fuming. almost as mad at her as i was at you. almost.

i'm sorry, evan. i really am. but she's thirty-two years old, we couldn't treat her like a kid anymore.

i turned on my heel, walked back towards my room and slammed the door. i couldn't deal with this.

80. the only one in the room.

i wasn't mad. of course i wasn't mad, i bought a new dress and some people actually pronounced my name right and you were in the corner playing your guitar and i ate a lot of cheese cubes and refused to talk to any reporters and you sold copies of that sort-of ep you recorded and of course i was happy, i'm wearing a new goddamned dress!

p.s., motherfucker:

when i said i didn't sleep with james, i meant that i didn't get to *fourth base* with james.

81. elsewhere.

when i woke up, manoel was gone, off to build another pool. more than thirty years in america and he's still doing fresh-off-the-boat jobs. leonor was making coffee, peering at the newspaper over the edge of her readers. fionna wove between my legs and ate the kibble i placed at her feet. my aunt passed me a cup of coffee and the sugar bowl. at least *someone* understands.

how long were you planning on staying here? she asked timidly.

i took a sip.

i don't know. a few months?

she made a face like she was about to throw up.

do you want to see melissa?

yes, i answered immediately.

i'll take you. but first — she reached under the sink and pulled out carpet spot-cleaner — *you're taking care of that.*

she pointed at the piss stain in the middle of the living room. i downed the rest of my coffee and started scrubbing.

i took a long shower, desperate for the steam to fog up my entire life. how do you dress to go see your paralyzed sister? i'm nearly thirty years old and my wardrobe is still ninety percent band shirts. something needs to change, but i don't want to actually *do* it.

the sun rose on the parkway as we drove, a strange pinkish-orange, and for the first time in a long time, i didn't think of you.

82. lines.

james found me in the bathroom, staring at a group of skinny girls doing cocaine.

hey, he whispered through an ajar door, afraid to actually come in. *you okay?*

is he still playing and selling his stupid cds at my event?

it's technically the library's event, he said.

i will pull your balls up your throat, i threatened. other people get sloppy drunk, i just get bitchy drunk. it's a power i've only used for evil, i'm afraid.

he opened the door wider. the model-types didn't notice.

evan, i know what we did was a mistake. but you came onto me. i'm not at fault here. but i don't want this to destroy our friendship.

oh please, it was just a blowjob, get over yourself.

evan, come on. i know you care about him. i mean, you've been together for more than a year now. you want him. you don't want me.

i looked at him, into his all-american blue eyes, and for a moment, maybe i did want him. he could be sweet and actually take me out on dates and not stay up until three in the morning insisting he's *writing new material.*

but i wouldn't wake to his face buried in my hair or have him name his guitar after me. he wouldn't make some brazilian-voodoo hangover cure the morning after or exaggerate his new jersey accent to make me giggle or help me put on complicated necklaces i shouldn't have bought or kiss the tip of my nose and call me *red*. because he wasn't you.

and i guess being with you is hard, but giving you up is even harder.

83. superglue.

it was a nice-looking place. pineview community, not too far from batsto. leonor pulled into a parking spot and unlocked my door.

go, she said.

what?

go. i'll wait here. she pulled a gossip magazine from her purse.

you're not going in?

you should talk to her alone. i'll visit her on sunday with manoel.

um. okay.

i got out of the car, pulled at my t-shirt, arched my back. my heart pounded as i walked in. it smelled like antiseptic. but more complicated that that. antiseptic with especially pungent shit underneath. there were dusty fake plants in the corner.

when i approached the desk, the receptionist looked up at me and hissed,

sir, i already told you, our oxycontin isn't for sale.

um, what?

oh, i'm sorry, she answered, blushing. *i must've thought you were someone else.*

i arched an eyebrow, looked around, felt like i was checking into the bates motel. it was eerily quiet.

um. yeah. i'm here to see melissa arinos.

your name? she looked towards her computer.

evan arinos. i'm her brother.

she's upstairs. jane will show you. she handed me a visitor badge. i put it in my pocket.

a woman in purple scrubs — was she actually a nurse? i couldn't tell — led me to an elevator. she attempted to make conversation. i just shook.

my sister was at the window, reading a book. *at least she can read,* i remember the physical therapist telling my aunt and uncle about a year afterwards. *that's something.*

i coughed a bit. she looked up and smiled. or at least she tried to.

evan, she said.

hey, missy. i came to visit you.

of course, when i think about why i *really* came to new jersey, i want to drown myself, so i'll just tell myself that i came to see her.

come. she tried to beckon with her hand. i understood what she meant. i sat on her bed — a real bed, not a hospital one. it was a nice room, i guess. kind of small, but she had a picture on the nightstand of the whole family together, at our wedding. you were in it, long white dress, the bump of something that never came to be. i nearly started crying.

lydia? my sister asked. she wanted to know where you were, i could tell. i let out a long breath.

we're... she's not here. we're taking a break, i guess.

melissa nodded, understanding. that's what people always forget—she can't say much, but she understands.

baby?

i sucked in a breath, bit my lip against the tears.

the baby's gone, melissa. it's gone.

she's gone. i never really know what to say. maybe we should've had a funeral. but who would we invite? what good does burying a half-formed chance do? at this point, people must've figured out that we only got married because it was what we had been conditioned to think was best.

melissa said nothing. she just looked at her lap, the tiny flowers on her skirt, the skin on her hands, still puckered from the grafts. she wore my mother's wedding ring on her right hand. i don't know what happened to my father's.

a nurse—attendant? assistant? she was wearing scrubs, too—came in, knocking on the doorframe.

drew's here to see you, melissa. can he come in?

yes, she said, because she can't nod. her neck never went back the right way.

a man walked in, his gait somewhat lopsided. his clothes were unkempt and he was cross-eyed, but melissa smiled. *really* smiled. he sat in the chair next to her, kissed her cheek, held her hand. my eyes widened. the nurse hovered in the doorway, hand over her heart.

hi, i said in his direction, holding out my hand to shake. *i'm evan, melissa's brother. i didn't know she had a boyfriend.*

nothing. he didn't even look my way. melissa's eyes met mine, but i couldn't tell what they were saying.

he's not being rude, the nurse said, leaning over and whispering. *he's severely autistic. he has trouble communicating.*

but he and my sister are... do they talk?

not much. but they've been very close ever since she came here. he's been here since he was eighteen. his parents just... weren't prepared, i guess.

are they, like, dating? for real?

well, they like watching tv together. cartoons, mostly. we're taking them to the mall soon. she wants some new shoes.

i stood up, grabbed the nurse by the arm, dragged her out into the hallway.

sir —

is she happy here? i asked, more forceful than i should've been.

what?

look, my aunt and uncle put her in here without telling me. she's my big sister and i want to make sure she's happy. is she happy with that guy?

of course she is, the nurse said. *they love being together. she's very participatory.*

participatory? this is a goddamned nursing home.

assisted living facility, she corrected. *your aunt and uncle made the right choice in bringing her here. she has a chance to socialize. be with other people. and when she first arrived, she did seem scared. she kept asking for you.*

for me? for evan?

mmhmm. you're very important to her. but here, she's able to meet more people who will be important to her. you can't just depend on one person for all your happiness.

but is she —

she's been doing great here. the physical therapist and speech therapist are both really impressed with her progress so far. she'll never be back to how she was before the accident, but we can help her improve. a lot.

i looked back over my shoulder, at her, at them. she was broken, and i guess she's on her way to being fixed, or at least a little closer.

maybe i can do it, too.

84. walking pneumonia.

you were packing up your guitar as the party dissolved, as i downed by fourth—fifth?—mojito and walked over to you.

hey, i said, or slurred. everything was fuzzy at the edges. you looked up. i don't know why i ever doubted that smile.

hey yourself. i stepped closer and tripped over my heels. you caught me, my fingers digging into your meaty italian-mafia forearms. i forget about that part of you, the *nunca parar* overshadowing the *mai smettere.*

whoa there. you stooped down a bit, looked me in the eyes. *fuck, evan, how drunk are you?*

i love you, you know that? i asked.

of course i do, you answered. *i love you too.*

more. you were supposed to say more.

come on, you said, helping me to my feet. *let's get you home.*

it was a warm spring night, as they were dying the river green. i threw up in the gutter and you held my hair back, kissing my knuckles when i came up for air. you looked straight into my eyes, as though you still believed in me.

i'm sorry, i said, shuddering. it wasn't even that cold.

i'm not mad, you answered. i didn't know if i was apologizing for getting drunk or for getting sick or for blowing james or for just existing and turning your life to shit. it didn't matter, because you took me upstairs, helped me into bed, took off my shoes. you kissed my forehead and wished me sweet dreams.

we're the water in each others' lungs, and i guess we're not going anywhere.

85. deleted numbers.

my aunt asked me to come shopping with her. i've always hated grocery stores, the soggy produce and the squeaky wheels on the carts and the raccoon-eyed girls i went to high school with at the checkout counter.

but i guess i needed to get out of the house. i had spent the past week locked in my room, trying to force fionna to spoon with me (is cat-scratch fever real? i need to google that), listening to the cranberries on repeat. i almost picked up my phone and texted you the lyrics. almost.

while leonor picked up ten-for-ten-dollars yogurt, i felt a tap on my shoulder. i turned around.

evan arinos! a rail-skinny guy in black jeans and an acme smock said, arms out wide.

hey, jon, i said after a split second of trying to remember who he was. i didn't stay long after graduation. wildwood to newark to philly to chicago. everyone had grown up without me.

jon leary used to be a fat kid. he still seemed like a horrible, horrible poser, like he had bought that t-shirt with the tiny holes already in it.

how have you been? i asked him.

great, man. finally moved out of my parents' place. what are you doing here? thought you were in chicago.

california, i corrected. *i'm just visiting.*

heard that album you put out. tight, man. real tight. did you see the review in alternative press?

i saw the three sentences they wrote about me in alternative press. they weren't terribly positive.

yeah. thanks. glad you like it.

leonor called my name, pointed towards the bread aisle. i made *hold on a minute* eyes, even though i didn't want to keep talking to him.

how long you here for?

not sure. a few more weeks, maybe.

well, we were gonna head over to ac on friday. stay the weekend. like, me, chris, justin, maybe heather… you wanna tag along?

i shrugged.

sure, why not?

we were probably gonna take the train. i'll text you the details. heather's cousin might be able to get us into a lower learning show.

i don't know, man, they never did much for me.

whatever. i saw 'em a few years ago. we can go to a casino.

eh.

come on, evan, you used to love going to ac.

yeah. i didn't know what else to say. gambling had lost its appeal once i had something i could actually lose. i already placed my bets on the wrong numbers, i don't need more proof.

so come with us. you haven't been here in years, man. don't you want to celebrate your album release with your friends?

i didn't have the heart to tell him that my only friend is you, and that you're probably on the phone with a divorce lawyer right now.

i bought a ticket to atlantic city.

i keep wondering what they actually did with her body.

86. ultimatums.

lazy sunday. sometimes you need a whole day to spend in your pajamas, eat cold pizza for breakfast, figure out where the other is ticklish. you kissed every inch of me, played connect-the-dots with the freckles across my upper arms. boyish.

i was sketching out a new painting—i think i've been reading too much about whistler—when you looked up from your music magazine.

we should get married.

i looked up, pencil suspended above the page.

what?

well, not like, right now. or right now. i don't know, forget i said it.

i sighed, put my sketchbook down. fionna rolled over in the patch of sunlight on the floor, swatting at floating dust.

weddings are expensive.

they don't have to be. we could just go to city hall.

i don't know if i'm really… ready for that. it's a big step.

i sound mean. of course i sound mean. stupid girl, stupid girl. twenty-six isn't that young to get married. if anything it was old, back in the day.

if you're not ready, i'm not gonna harass you, you promised. i'm not sure if i believed you. i wanted to, but no one ever really asks me what i want. *just forget i said it.*

i put my sketchbook on the floor and moved to your side of the couch, straddling your hips and taking off your glasses. so much seemed like that first night, that first chance.

i will marry you. someday, i promised in a whisper. *we can just be us for now.*

my pinky locked with yours, and for a little while, *forever* didn't seem that scary.

87. born as.

i called a cab on thursday, while my aunt was at her book club. back to pineview. i had seen melissa a few more times since arriving. we went to batsto village last sunday, and i couldn't stop thinking of that time we came to glassboro for christmas, when we walked through the forest, hand in hand, boots crunching in the snow. it's august, and i've never felt colder.

i said hi to the receptionist, walked upstairs to melissa's room. drew wasn't there, and somehow, that made me feel calmer.

i walked in, and she smiled as best she could manage. she had her new shoes from the mall—slip-on vans, just like yours.

evan, she said. always happy to see me. maybe the last one.

i sat down.

melissa, i need to tell you something. her eyes grew wide. she didn't know what to expect.

lydia? my flesh crawled at the name. *divorce?*

no. i took her hands in mine. *melissa, my wife's name is evan. not lydia. i'm evan, and she's evan too. do you understand?*

yes, she said, but i wasn't sure. i just needed people to understand. i just wanted you to understand, from wherever you were—i want to be *evan and evan.* i want to be *us.*

88. like a lamb.

the first warm day of spring, finally. you came home from work, beaming, and you put down your bag.

put on your shoes, we're going to the navy pier.

really?

yeah. hot dogs are on me, you said.

i put on my sneakers, picked up my purse. it's so much easier to be spontaneous when the sun is shining. and it's harder to be mad at you when it's warm enough to forgo a jacket.

on the el, you put an arm around my shoulders, kissed my cheek, told me i was beautiful.

and i guess, it's easier to say yes when you're touching me and not your guitar.

89. the losing end.

casinos are terrifying. i put a few quarters in a few slot machines, walked away with forty bucks or so, but i hate that there's no windows. if it weren't for my phone, i'd have no fucking idea what time it was.

i resorted to my usual plan: i ditched my friends, sat at the bar. for some reason, i ordered a mojito. you like mojitos. i don't know why, i felt like i was drinking toothpaste.

and suddenly, from across the bar, there was a double-take, a head-tilt of hesitation.

evan? a woman called out from the other side, across the stacks of cheap liquor bottles, voice ringing off the inverted glasses hanging from the ceiling. *evan arinos?*

i looked up from the cocktail napkin where i had scribbled lyrics. not that they'd ever amount to anything.

oh, hey, lucy. what are you doing here?

just... she stood up, walked around to my side, sat in the stool next to me. *well, i got dragged into my cousin's bachelorette party. i think she's still at the tropicana. wow, cool tattoos.*

oh, yeah. thanks.

so how are you, it's been forever!

she play-punched my forearm, and i wanted to real-punch her back.

good, i guess. i'm living in l.a. now.

cool. oh, i heard about your album! i haven't been able to listen to it yet, though.

well, my entire fuckin' garage is full of copies, just hit me up, i said, laughing, trying to be funny, but i really just wanted to cry. *but you can stream the whole thing, it's not, like, piracy or anything.*

awesome. i'll be sure to check it out. she took a sip of her cosmo.

so, what are you up to?

she shrugged. *beauty school was kinda a bust. i'm a receptionist, but i'm probably gonna go back to school. for something. i really thought i'd have it figured out by now, but… well, you know.*

yeah. i stared down my glass, watching the mint leaves float around and around. *i know.*

she let out a long sigh.

i've heard the tables at the tropicana have better odds. and if i see one more cocktail waitress in a cowboy hat i'm gonna move to canada. you wanna come with?

she had gotten hotter since high school, i was lonely, and i guess by the time we stumbled into her hotel room, sloppy with hard liquor, we were both looking for some sort of jackpot.

everything feels like you, and then it doesn't.

90. fisheye lens.

nothing quite like art block. you were at work, and i was hanging upside-down off the bed, trying to see everything differently. it wasn't really working. all i knew was that i was sick of the couch-sized landscapes.

i looked out the window, sipping maybe my sixth cup of green tea, head slumped. nothing seemed interesting. my day didn't become worth it until you came home.

i started painting our bed. maybe as just a warmup. i bit my lips as i tried to get all the folds right, capture the different shades of gray in fionna's fur. she stood up, stretched up like a halloween decoration, and jumped to the floor.

when you came home, i was stitching pieces of my canvas back together, still wet with oil paint, creating something that wasn't quite what it used to be.

and maybe, just maybe, i was okay with that.

91. hair of the dog.

nothing quite like a walk of shame. or a train ride of shame. i returned from atlantic city on sunday morning, while my aunt and uncle were at church. oh, the perks of living with hardcore catholics. there was a strange silence, a loneliness i couldn't place. it wasn't necessarily because of you. or because of lucy. i'm empty, and i'm not sure what can fill it.

i drank a shot of rum from manoel's stash in the back of the pantry, and i fell asleep, curled up on the couch, fionna at my feet. i woke to find a blanket and a cup of coffee waiting.

manoel and leonor were in the kitchen, making coxinhas, when i walked in.

how was atlantic city? my aunt asked.

i guess you didn't hit the jackpot. otherwise you could buy us a summer house in jericoacoara, my uncle added.

i took a gulp of coffee. the clock above the stove said three-twelve.

evan? you okay? oh tadinho. go lie back down, leonor said, steering me back towards the couch.

uncle manoel? i asked over my shoulder.

yes? he asked.

tomorrow after you come home from work, will you teach me how to drive?

my aunt looked concerned, eyes darting between me and her husband, but she said nothing.

sure, manoel answered. *we've got some leftover palm hearts, you want a snack?*

92. the break.

when i came out of the shower, you were on the phone, scribbling furiously. i reached towards my bathrobe, lying on the floor, and towel-dried my hair. the dye was fading fast. fuck.

okay. thank you so much. i'll see you soon. bye. thank you.

i tied the sash of my bathrobe tight, reached for my mousse.

who was that? i asked.

babe, start looking at lofts in gold coast, we're gonna be out of this shitty apartment soon.

what's wrong with humboldt? i gave you a confused look. *what's going on?*

i got a show at exit. exit! kiss this place goodbye, we can go live in fucking evanston!

northwestern students scare you.

exit! evan, fucking exit!

i could see the expectation in your eyes, because you believed any punk act from here that ever made it started at exit. you've reached your holy grail, your mountaintop.

so i said *that's great, honey, i'm so proud of you,* and i hugged you tight, because i have nothing else, really.

93. independence day.

i landed in l.a. just as the sun was setting, a cool september night. i had three weeks' worth of manoel's driving lessons under my belt, and i was going for my california permit as soon as i was settled in. i'd have to find someone with a valid cali license to practice with, though. the only person i knew with one of those was you.

i took the bus back home, walked in the door, let fionna out. everything was exactly as i had left it, and i probably should've thrown out the mustard before leaving.

i sat on the bed — our bed, my bed? just *the* bed, i guess — and ran my palm over the bedspread, the quilt your mother made us as a housewarming present. no one ever thought we were going to get married, so we got the wedding presents when we arrived in north hollywood. it seemed stupid. i mean, this place is still rented, it's not like anything was permanent.

except us. we were supposed to be permanent.

i took my phone out of my pocket, taking a deep breath, thumbs suspended above the screen. i dialed on the exhale.

neil rogers.

it's evan. i'm done.

what? he shouted.

i hung up and turned my phone off before he could call back.

it's good to be home. maybe it's finally starting to feel like that.

94. authenticity.

i kind of hate mosh pits. they're hot and gross and degrading, honestly. but of course you had to play at a club with no goddamned backstage, so here i am, up against the barricade like a french revolutionary, covered in other people's sweat. who even moshes to acoustic punk?

then again, who doesn't?

when i saw you at that coffeeshop (over a year ago, shit), you seemed so nervous. but now, you played the crowd, smiling and laughing as they shouted the lyrics back at you. there weren't that many people there, but i knew, from the way they cheered, clapped, sweat for you, that they cared. pop stars play to arenas with thousands, and lots of people there don't care. they're casual fans, their girlfriend dragged them there. they just want to make sure their kid doesn't get hurt. they don't know the words. they don't even know the song titles. but here, in this club with maybe the grossest bathrooms i've seen outside of hurricane katrina coverage, i know they care.

i do, too.

95. used to be.

the guys i recorded the album with came over, along with a few six-packs and some boxes from little ceasars. i guess i do miss the pizza in chicago. and new jersey. the only thing l.a. can do well is mexican. and maybe korean.

so, what's next? my bass player asked, flicking through the tv listings. *y'know, after we find this kid a piece of ass.* he clapped my shoulder and i flipped him off. just because he's three years older than me doesn't make me a *kid*.

hey, man, that's not cool, the drummer said. still with that shake in his leg. god, i want to punch him. *evan went through some pretty rough stuff.*

is the divorce official yet? the bass player asked.

let's release stuff independently, i suggested. *at least try to. i mean, radiohead could do it.*

yeah, but they have money. i went broke paying for this shitty pizza, the other guitarist said. we don't talk about him.

it's called the internet, retard, the drummer answered, mouth full.

everyone waited for my *hey, my sister's retarded,* but she isn't, really. she might be the smartest, sanest, strongest person i know.

we can do it. and we don't have to listen to the record company's bullshit. and we're never gonna end up on another gross summer emo tour again. we're not opening for a christian metal band or whatever that was.

oh my god, that was the worst, the drummer — okay, his name is rick, i don't know why i was trying to keep that from you. *like, who the fuck invited them?*

those tours suck. the lineup sucks, the squealing fangirls who are just there to see some fucking boyband suck. i just like the free food, nate the other guitarist said.

we all laughed, even me, and fionna jumped on my lap and licked the grease off my fingers, and i guess, for the first time, i felt like i was going to be okay.

96. decluttering.

ah, spring cleaning. we finally got around to selling my old roommate's furniture on craigslist (*i don't want to use a website that has its own lifetime movie,* i argued, but you won. you always win) and now we were trying to organize everything. you turned on your favorite vinyl and we opened the windows wide, shouting the lyrics out the screens. what's our age again?

and while you were out, picking up our chinese takeout dinner, i figured my phone could use some spring cleaning too. i deleted apps i didn't use, blurry pictures of fionna that weren't social-media-worthy. and as i heard the lock turn behind me, i clicked *contacts,* scrolled straight to *james stone,* and i deleted that too.

97. small steps.

i woke to my phone ringing. i rolled over, picked it up, half-expecting it to be someone i actually wanted to talk to. but it was my aunt and uncle's home number. i sat up, rubbing the sleep from my eyes.

hello?

hello, anjinho, are you in l.a.? my aunt asked.

yes. um. where else would i be?

i could almost hear her scowling.

i just wanted to make sure you were okay.

i'm fine.

have you talked to — she hesitated *— evan?*

i gave her the same talk i gave melissa. i wanted to drill it into people's heads. us us us. i wanted to be us.

not yet. i'm just… waiting to see. how everything works out.

actually, i thought about calling you all the time. inviting you over for dinner. meeting you up for coffee. or just finding out where you were and showing up, begging for forgiveness, begging for it all back. we could have another baby, if that was what you wanted. you could come back here. without you, this place is just a bunch of walls and a staircase and a goddamned avocado tree. nothing else.

do you have your license?

no, not yet. just my permit. but i'll take my test soon.

i'll need a car, though. you still have the car. i don't even know if you're in l.a. oh well. i have money. i think?

good. i'm glad you're better.

i wasn't sure if i was better. i wasn't crying myself to sleep anymore, so i guess i'm making progress.

yeah. thanks for letting me stay.

it's not a problem. melissa wants you to come for thanksgiving.

i'll try.

that's all i really can do now. try.

98. sea legs.

you called me while i was heading back from the art store, carrying rolled canvases under my arm and lugging a bag full of paints.

hey, babe. you still at work?

yeah, but it's dead. we're going out for dinner tonight. you sounded very excited. almost too excited.

like, red lobster out, or gino's east out, or, like, top chef runner-up restaurant out, or…

it's a surprise.

i stopped on the sidewalk.

evan, do i have to go buy pantyhose? i asked, stomping a bit.

nah. just… dress like the rest of your life is starting.

you hung up, and i froze. after a while, i turned into a bodega and asked the guy behind the lotto counter if i could use their bathroom. he said yes.

i may or may not have thrown up in the sink. i can't tell you, because that would ruin the goddamned *surprise*.

99. rain in paper cups.

after i passed my driver's test, i rented a car and drove to venice beach. i don't know why. three years here, and i've never been. i haven't been to a lot of places, actually, i don't know who to blame that on.

parking was a bit of a nightmare. maybe *that's* the real reason i avoided learning how to drive. but i eventually found a spot, and i started walking towards the ocean, following the salt air. i wasn't even that far from home, but it felt like another goddamn country. drum circles and surfers and *space*, so much freakin' *space*. for the first time in three years, i was in southern california and i felt like i could actually breathe. i walked along the sidewalk, skaters swerving around me, strolling past smoke shops and sushi restaurants. oil drums as garbage cans, tourists taking pictures of seagulls.

i took off my sneakers, rolled up my jeans a bit, and stepped into the ocean, felt the sand between my toes. the cool water, perfect on this indian-summer day. then again, summer never really ends here. never. and maybe that was what threw us off. but there's no reason it has to keep us apart forever. i remember our first night in the house, when we sat on the back porch and drank wine coolers because we couldn't afford champagne, trying to see the stars through the smog, when you reached over and linked your pinky with mine.

we'll be happy here, you said.

yeah, i said. *hey, i think that's an avocado tree. maybe we'll make guacamole.*

you looked over and smiled, permeating the darkness. i remember that smile. it's almost as though i'm haunted by it.

we'll be happy here, we'll be happy here. i practically chanted it in my head as i walked back to the car. and across the street from the parking lot, coming out of a tattoo parlor, i saw you. or i thought i did. i wasn't sure. you wouldn't wear shorts that short, and you wouldn't ever get a tattoo (you want to be buried in a jewish cemetery, you repeated over and over, as i added more and more to my arms until they were eventually covered. you half-assed hanukkah. *hanukkah.*)

but that person coming out of the tattoo parlor had your hair, full and bouncy and wavy, that shade of dark red that everyone knew came from a bottle but somehow looked natural anyway. *dark henna mist,* i think it said on that box i found in the bathroom. but it wasn't dark henna mist. it was evan lydia zahner, my love, my life, my wife. still. it was you. i knew it was you, with that tattoo cover wrapped around your thigh, with that hair, with that split-second glance over your shoulder, perhaps to let me know that you were you, and i was i, and that we were we, somewhere in this universe or another.

100. molly bloom.

i knew where we were going as soon as we got on the el towards wrigley. but i didn't say anything, because i knew you wanted the surprise to stay, to stick. i guess i dressed like the rest of my life was starting, in my favorite blouse, short sleeves with the little Prussian-blue flowers, and a blue skirt. you wore jeans and some band t-shirt. jeans. *jeans.* it was eighty degrees already. this must've been important.

i faked surprise at seeing the shawarma restaurant better than i fake orgasms. oh. whoops. i guess that was a secret too.

part of me didn't want to go in. i mean, i was *fired*. for spending too much time with you, if you recall. but you held my hand as we walked inside, and i suddenly felt safe. protected. and i guess i felt like i mattered, to someone.

no one recognized me, thank god. seemed like they had gotten a lot of new waitresses, anyway. you ordered a turkey shawarma and mint tea. i went for the hummus platter, because, again, eighty degrees. too hot for grilled anything.

wow, it hasn't changed a bit, i said, looking around. you reached across the table, grabbed my hand.

this was the table i used to sit at. this table was in your section.

yeah, it was. i didn't mean to sound disoriented. i was just feeling like i was in one of those dreams where you're falling, falling, falling and you wake up right before you hit the ground. i was about to hit the ground, shatter, no more evan.

hey, babe, are you okay? you asked. *you seem kinda… i thought you would like this. seeing where we met.*

i moved my hand out of your grip, tucked my hair behind my ears, took a deep breath. you *would* break big news to me to me in public where i couldn't make a scene. because heaven forbid i ever lose my temper. heaven forbid my emotions fall out of the *acceptable* range. heaven forbid —

evan, are you proposing? i asked in much calmer than i felt. *is that why you brought me here, to ask me to marry you?*

you crinkled your eyebrows, gave me a puzzled look.

oh god, did you take me here to break up? because jesus, evan — my voice cracked and i stopped, folding my hands and looking down at my lap. *i'm sorry. i know i've been jumpy.*

it's okay. you reached across the table again, put a thumb underneath my chin, tilted it up. i still like when you do that, even if it is infantilizing. that's the thing with you. for every annoying thing you do, there are ten, twenty, maybe a hundred things that you do that i can't live without. you remind me of that picture i saw on the internet once, of people who were struck my lightning and have these beautiful, bolt-shaped scars on their bodies, wrapped around them like tracery in a gothic church. you're painful, but you leave the good scars. the one i not only live with, but wear proudly.

okay, i was gonna wait until dessert to do this, but — you paused to take a deep breath — *some guy saw me at the exit show, and he's starting a record company, and he wants me to sign with him. for an ep or two, first, and then maybe a full-length. y'know, if it gets off the ground.*

oh my god. oh my god, evan, that's amazing!

yeah. yeah. you looked down at the table. i knew there was something else. there had to be. i bit my lip a little, sighed.

is there a catch? i think there's a catch, evan.

you looked up at the ceiling, then at me. you were nervous. and i guess i was catching it.

it's in los angeles. and he wants me to come out there. he got me a job in the house band of another company for the time being, and my first day is august first. it's steady. it's a paycheck. but it's in los angeles.

los angeles. california.

i know, i know. it's a big deal. and i should've told you before saying yes. i know. i'm sorry.

honey, don't apologize. it's okay. it's your career.

yeah. i know long-distance will be hard, but —

long-distance? are you fucking insane? i asked.

wha —

i'm coming with you, i answered, and i was sure. *sure* sure, as the sun will rise.

huh?

i'm coming with you to california. i can be a painter out there. or a waitress, more likely. i'm not reducing us to skype calls. i'm going with you.

really?

of course. i'm not going anywhere. but please, let's hold off on all that gross adult stuff for now. i want to be able to rent a car before i have to go wedding dress shopping, please.

you laughed, and i laughed, and it all felt so goddamn *real*, like i could bottle it up, sell it, dab it behind my ears.

dully noted. but you're serious, you'll really come with me?

it was then that i knew you weren't just the best i could do — you were the best, period.

it was then that i finally understood my bobeshi's old adage — it's better to try and fix something than throw it away.

and it was then that i held my pinky out, waiting for you to follow.

101. pinky swore.

i was making coffee in my boxer shorts when i heard a knock on the door. fionna, startled, ran upstairs. she hadn't really been the same since coming back from new jersey. baby steps.

i walked to the door, forgot to look through the peephole (the ultimate living-in-l.a. sin), and i saw you. really you, not that maybe-vision from venice beach a few days ago. that hair, that freckled skin. you were wearing your favorite blue dress, but it looked a little dirty. there was color on your skin, sticking out from under the hem. a bird? i guess it wasn't important.

hey, you said.

um. hi. hey. yeah. reduced to an awkward teenager in your presence. fuck. *how are you – um, how've you been?*

good, i guess. i, um… i heard you had been away for a while, and then i heard you were back, and i just wanted to say hi. you were trying to act like you didn't see me in venice. but i knew. we both knew. *and figure out a time to talk.*

about… don't say *the divorce*. don't say *the divorce*.

just to like, catch up. i mean, just… you paused to push your hair out of your eyes. you were wearing your ring. and i was wearing mine. i don't know how you got yours; i kept them on the dresser when i left. and yet, i knew anyway.

we can talk now. i don't have anywhere to be. you want coffee? i'm making some now.

the tiniest of smiles, like the flash of iridescence off butterfly wings.

sure.

you walked inside, not too stiff, looking around, remembering how everything was. i hadn't even touched the nursery, the crib and everything still in it. i'd get there.

i poured you a cup, in your college mug. it stayed here. nearly everything did.

did you go to wisconsin? i asked. we stood at opposite sides of the kitchen island, afraid to get too close. but i wanted to press myself to you until i didn't know where i ended and you began. i wanted to turn back the last year, make everything better. but i guess it can't get better until it gets worse.

yeah, you answered. *for a few weeks. and you went to new jersey?*

yeah. i saw my aunt and uncle and melissa.

how's she?

good. she's in an assisted living place now.

oh, really? you seemed concerned.

she's doing well there, though. she actually met a guy.

well, good for her. you took a sip. you smiled a little. don't think i didn't see.

where have you been staying? i asked. *y'know, since you got back?*

friends' places, you answered. *i sold the car. it was hard, i guess. but i'm looking at places in westwood.*

cool.

your eyes drifted towards the window.

holy shit, i don't believe it.

huh?

look, you said, pointing. *an avocado.*

we both walked towards the window. sure enough, there was an avocado at the end of one of the branches. not too big, but dark green and ripe-looking.

wow, i said.

we always said it would never happen, you answered. *let's go check it out.*

you walked out the back door with childlike curiosity, alice down the rabbithole. i followed, unsure, but sure. nothing is certain, and maybe that's what makes life beautiful.

it dangled low enough that i could reach up and touched it with my fingertips. for some reason, i expected a snake to come slithering down the tree trunk and issue a warning. we stood side-by-side, looked up at it, then at each other, then back at it. the air seemed to whisper: *us, us, us.*

i leaned over a little.

wanna eat it?

About The Author

Shea Warner grew up in New Jersey and is a graduate of Kenyon College. She now lives in London with her family.

Printed in Great Britain
by Amazon